GRAND NATIONAL

John R. Tunis

William Morrow and Company
New York 1973

Printed in the United States of America.

Library of Congress Catalog Card Number 73-4930

ISBN 0-688-20090-7
ISBN 0-688-30090-1 (lib. bdg.)

1 2 3 4 5 77 76 75 74 73

*To Thomas H. McKoy,
who won the Grand National in 1969
with his horse Highland Wedding.*

Gallant horse, gallant owner.

Grand National

By the Same Author

1

The room was large and comfortable, with a lived-in feeling, showing the traces of money and the things money can buy: old furniture, pictures, an Oriental rug. Over the fireplace hung the painting of a bay mare, posed, conventional. A silver plate at the bottom explained that the horse was Dusty Miller, winner of the 1952 Maryland Hunt Cup, ridden by J.I.B. Cobb, Esq.

On the various tables were trophies of every kind: silver cigarette boxes, photographs of horses in silver frames, silver cups large and small.

Shelves on two sides of the room were lined with books, giving it a warm appearance. On close examination these books turned out to be all about horses and hunting: *Fifty Years with the Quorn, The History of Steeplechasing, Saddle and Equitation.*

The young man across the room slumped into his easy chair until he was reclining on his spine. He had a mass of tawny hair. His father sat opposite, asking questions. Both were tense, their voices sharp and bitter.

"But Stan, you must have known your thesis was due. What happened?"

"Oh, Dad! Why should I break my neck cranking out a useless thesis? So I could graduate and join the rat race you've been in for thirty years? No thanks. I told you how I felt, but you never listened." He rose, tall, thin, with long legs. Then, seeing the pain on his father's face, he said, "All right, Dad. It's just that I want something more helpful than the things I studied at college."

"But Stanley, last year you were going for honors in history." The father felt stunned by the suddenness of his son's decision to leave school.

"I gave it up. How would you feel, Dad, if someone asked you to spend six months working on the origins of power in English town and village life in 1655?"

The father hesitated. The objection sounded reasonable, but the boy had thrown away his future without consulting him. He doesn't really know what he wants. Except to ride that horse.

The boy sank back into his chair. "When that topic was suggested, I walked out of the professor's room. Riding is a damn sight more *meaningful* than college."

"Stan, I doubt that your mother would have been happy to see you a gentleman rider." The older man spoke with an edge in his voice.

A silence settled over the room. Her death from leukemia the previous year cut into them both. "Maybe. But I know one thing. She wanted me to be myself. She often told me so."

"Perhaps," said his father coldly. "But it seems to me that you simply find it more fun to ride Quicksilver at some race meeting in Virginia than to dig down to get an honors degree at college. Aren't you using that horse as a cop-out?"

The boy flushed, and Jack Cobb sat thinking how much worse the situation was than he imagined. Maybe he should never have given Stan that wonderful horse. This boy presents the il-

11

lusion of maturity, Cobb thought, but how awful to be so incapable of compromise.

"Stan, if you leave college now to ride that horse, your name will get back to your draft board right away."

"With my number, sixteen, I'm elected no matter what I do." He got to his feet again, tall, fit, and implacable. "But I want some good races before I go. Y'know, Dad, I had Quicksilver over the fences for an hour today. I believe I have a chance at the Hunt Cup next week—if old Smitty leaves me alone. And if I win, I might try for the National in England."

How can he make such a suggestion with the draft facing him? Cobb was aghast. And at this time. It had been the worst of weeks for the firm of Cobb and Stevenson. Rumors of its bankruptcy were all over town. Customers were even asking for their securities. The older man rose wearily, a hand involuntarily passing over his forehead. "I have a hard day tomorrow. I must get to bed. Lock up for me, please, Stan."

Up the stairs he went in the silent, lonely house. What would the next day bring? Yet his thoughts were on the boy. What will become of him? What on earth will become of him?

2

He knew perfectly well why Stanley had chosen to sleep away from home the night before the Maryland Hunt Cup. After the scene of the previous week, Stanley did not want to risk another argument, so had phoned to say that he was going to stay with his roommate, who lived at Pikesville on the edge of the course.

On Saturday Jack Cobb rose early. He knew well enough that Stanley had a great chance to win. After all, who was better over those fences? With a magnificent horse on a sunny spring day with the sky blue above, he felt his boy was better than anyone in the race.

At six thirty in the morning he was on the road, noticing that the signs leading to the course were up already. In a few minutes the whole expanse of the race stretched out before him. The Maryland Hunt Cup was the oldest as well as the stiffest cross-country timber race in the nation. Immediately Jack Cobb noticed something else; the rain-soaked turf was shimmering in the dew of early spring.

Jack walked slowly along, testing the turf at each fence, recalling the history of each jump. There was the third—five rails and five feet high —where trouble began. The sixth was also dangerous. At the seventh, an old friend had gone over the neck of his horse and died from the fall. The eighth was another uphill jump, and hard. He had heard of many horses breaking their neck at it. One of his own mounts had caught a rail and brought him down there a number of years ago. The thirteenth, almost five feet in height, was called the Union Memorial, because it sent so many riders to the hospital of that same name in Baltimore.

Jack walked along, studying the terrain, locating the best place from which to take each jump. The quickest way around was to stay as close to the inside as possible. He noticed that the ground was much softer inside, but still he felt that Quicksilver would be better there.

That afternoon, over a course only four hundred yards shorter than the Grand National in England, Stan had to face the best jumpers and leading amateur riders in the country. Beyond the two-mile circle stretched twenty fences, mostly constructed out of West Virginia chestnut. Five feet in height, the rails were formidable and grim. Few horses ever broke one and remained standing.

At that moment Jack noticed a determined figure approaching. It was P.J.M. Smith, old Smitty himself, clean-shaven so that Jack noticed his jowls were blue in the crisp morning air. Dressed immaculately in tailored jodhpurs and a smart sports coat, Marshall Smith made everyone else feel shabby. He was an older and more celebrated rider, a well-to-do banker who lived outside Baltimore. Despite the many years he had ridden in this race, he never had won it. All winter he had worked and trained faithfully, bringing his big mare, Norman Blood, into perfect form. His racing days were ending, so he had to win this year or not at all. Everyone in racing knew Smitty was a rough, aggressive rider, taking chances, giving away nothing, fighting every inch of the way to get the maximum from his mount.

"Morning, Jack." Was there a patronizing touch of contempt in his tone, as his eager eyes swept over Jack's baggy pants and patched coat?

"Morning, Smitty. Nice day after all the rain this week."

· "Yes. The turf should be fairly well dried out by this afternoon." Smitty spoke with authority.

Jack's eyes moved over the grass. "Likely it may be on the slow side, though."

"I guess you're right. You know," he said suddenly, "I always felt you made a mistake on that horse of Stanley's."

Last week there had been moments when Jack came close to hating his boy for the risk that he was taking with his future. But to hear someone speak slightingly of Stan's chances was unbearable. He hardly trusted himself to speak. At last he said, "I guess you know the kind of rider Stan is, Smitty, and I got him the best horse I've seen in a long while. After all, I'm a fairly good judge of horseflesh. You remember in 1960. . . ."

His words struck home. In 1960, Cobb had been ahead of Smitty at every jump. Cobb saw Smith go pale, but his expression never changed. With a quick "See you later" he strode off.

I hope Stan beats the life out of him, Cobb thought furiously.

A half hour later, having walked the entire circle carefully, he moved along to the big red barn up the hillside. The stableboy was leading horses outside and greeted him cheerily. "Morning, Mr. Cobb. How's your son feeling today?"

"Oh, he's all right. How's the horse?"

"Raring to go, Mr. Cobb, but everybody's talking about how Mr. Smith is dead sure to win the race. Mister Stanley has sure got his hands full, and that's the truth."

Jack nodded and stepped inside the barn. Immediately a familiar neigh came down the rows of the stalls, and he could distinguish the stamp of Quicksilver's hooves, crisp and expectant. Slowly he approached the stall. Quicksilver was a big bay gelding with fine quarters, good shoulders, and a marvelous head, which he extended as Jack came toward him. On being touched, the horse at once responded, as if to say that he realized what Jack felt at this moment.

Cobb had bought the horse, as a foal, from

a country doctor outside Lexington, Kentucky. The sire was a Thoroughbred once entered in the Derby; the mare had won the Colonial Cup in South Carolina. As a young horse, Quicksilver had good lines, and Cobb had told the story of his purchase many times. "Imagine, a horse like Quicksilver for a hundred and fifty bucks."

Now this beast was a trained racer. As Jack stroked the animal's neck, he felt him nuzzle his arm. Quicksilver wanted to be liked; he had a real feeling for Jack and also for Stanley. For a moment Jack stood there, stroking Quicksilver's neck. He felt the immense spirit of the animal, the fire and drive deep inside. With what Stan had learned about racing, he should do well with the horse.

Two horses had been scratched that morning and another had turned up lame, so the field was reduced to seven. Yet all seven were top riders. Buzz Scott, Stan's senior by five years, had ridden two Hunt Cup races on an eight-year-old named Jet Plane; Peter Lambeth on Ground Mist had pushed the winner of the previous year. Then, of course, there was Smitty.

The horses and riders worked their way

through the crowd inside the circle made of red-painted snow fence, people standing ten feet deep on both sides of the start. As Stan moved in a few yards down, Jack could hear the boy's name coming from that sea of faces around him.

"Have a good ride, Stanley. Have a good ride, Stan boy."

Quicksilver reared slightly and moved nervously as Jack Cobb appeared at his side, took the bridle, and led the horse, with Stanley astride him, a few yards down the track and away from the crowd.

"Now, son, let him run his race and get over the fences his own way. He'll have the stuff when you need it. And just remember that the inside can be worth more than a half length or more. I've walked the course, and I know what I'm saying."

Stanley looked down, frowning. "Yes, Dad, sure. But I walked the course, too, later than you did. It's softer on the inside, and Quicksilver doesn't do well in that kind of stuff."

Suddenly Stanley's name boomed out over the loudspeaker. "Mr. Cobb, Mr. Stanley Cobb, Number 5. At the judges' stand, please."

Still Jack held onto the reins. "And whatever

you do, watch our friend. Oh, he's tricky all right. He'll try to cut you off at the slightest chance, because he knows that you can beat him in a fair race. But you won't have any trouble, son. You're going to be okay."

"Right, Dad, right."

Jack could feel that Stanley didn't want to hear any more of his suggestions. The boy was patting Quicksilver's neck, trying to soothe him. Obviously Stanley was tense and trying not to flare out at his father. Jack knew the boy wished he would clear out and let him ride the race his own way, but he couldn't seem to stop himself talking.

The loudspeaker blasted over the crowd. "Mr. Cobb. Mr. Stanley Cobb. At the judges' stand, please."

Still Jack held onto the reins. He had to get through to his son. "Stan, I know what I'm talking about."

"All right, Dad. Of course, you've ridden far more than I have. Only I know more about this horse than you do."

The loudspeaker blared again. Abruptly and angrily Stanley left his father holding the reins. Jack Cobb watched him shove through the crowd past Marshall Smith, who stood with his hands casually in his pockets. His boots were perfection, his blue silks glistened in the afternoon. He was tanned, fit, and looked unbeatable. Stan squeezed his way outside the rails to the judges' enclosure, and Smitty, slapping his whip against his boots, nodded at him. Jack noted with satisfaction that Stan ignored the other man.

Obviously the starter's question was a minor one, for very soon Jack could see the boy edging back through the crowd toward him. He squeezed through and without a word put his foot in the irons and vaulted up. How like me at his age he is, thought Jack as he watched his son.

Jack Cobb watched his boy intently as he took Quicksilver to the barrier. Perhaps this race would be Stan's last for a long while. Buzz Scott brought Jet Plane sharply under control.

Then they were off.

Jack wondered if Stan would follow his advice. Somehow he thought not. And perhaps the boy was right. Maybe the turf was too soft on the inside today. Quicksilver was a heavy horse and might not do well on the inside. Dear God, help him to place at least, Jack thought. He's simply got to place.

Seven horses, weighing almost three and a half tons, jammed into the first fence, and together they were all over it. Then Jet Plane, beautifully handled by Buzz Scott, took a challenging position.

Jack Cobb had found a position on the crest of the hill, where the entire course lay at his feet, each fence distinct and visible. For a moment he lost the leaders in his glasses. Then someone near him in the crowd remarked, "Did you see him bump Stanley at that last fence? Just as they were about to go up, too."

From above Jack Cobb caught the field in his glasses once more, watching Stanley as he came down. The boy controlled the horse well, and then tore on, taking the next fence faultlessly.

"That was rough," said someone. "Always the same with Smitty. He has to win."

Suddenly a horse stumbled and took a downer. Jack Cobb, watching anxiously, saw that Stanley was staying on the outside. The boy is playing it safe. And what's more, he's cutting Smitty down. No, he isn't. Yes, he is too. The heart of the father jumped. He's gaining. There's no question of it.

They were once around now, and the field,

with Smitty leading, was scattered out behind. They crossed the tanbark spread over the Tufton Road, and there were not too many fences left. But Stanley was coming on. With a burst of speed, he brought his horse to a challenging position. Jack Cobb leaned forward tensely.

"Keep cool, boy. Keep cool," said Jack to himself, as Stan raced in from the far outside. He swung up to Jet Plane and set out for Smitty. Was there still time? Watch the old bastard. Stan surged past Jet Plane and Ground Mist as though each were standing still, and Jack saw him drawing closer to Smitty.

Together the two animals rose in the air. And then Jack saw the older man below using the whip furiously. Now Stan was up to Norman Blood's girth. Now he was gaining by inches. They came toward the roaring crowd on each side of the red snow fence. Stanley seemed as cool as possible.

They entered the stretch absolutely even. But surely Stan was gaining by inches. All at once Jack realized the surge and pull of Quicksilver. He could hear the beating of Smitty's whip above the roar of the crowd. Suddenly Jack saw that the other horse could do no more. Smitty's face was red and contorted with rage, as he lashed Norman Blood with fury, but the animal had reached her limit. Imperceptibly at first, then faster and faster, Smitty fell back. The noise of the whip receded. All at once there was the finish, and the shrieking crowd was all that could be heard.

Up on the hillside, Jack never moved. Then he took off the gray cap he always wore at race meetings and held it silently in the air. Did anyone ever want to win a horse race as much as he did that afternoon? Ever?

3

The prediction of his father the week before the
Maryland Hunt Cup that Stanley's name would
soon get back to his draft board proved exact.
Within a few weeks he was taking basic training
in a camp in New Jersey. Next he was transferred
to Vietnam.

Then word came that he had been wounded.
Then, three days later, that he had died in a
hospital. Nothing heroic, not killed in action or
flying in a helicopter to save someone's life. No,
none of that. Merely a native in black pajamas

on a scooter roaring up the Avenue de la Victoire, the main artery of Saigon, with a tommy gun concealed under a raincoat. Passing several G.I.'s grouped on a corner, he stopped quietly, put out one foot to steady himself, flipped his raincoat aside, uncovered his weapon, and carefully sprayed them, attentively and accurately. When they tumbled to the ground, he shoved his weapon under the flapping raincoat and zoomed off into the dust and distance before anyone could catch up with him.

Same old thing, said the M.P.'s, who came running up at the sound of the fusillade. Result: two soldiers dead immediately, four badly wounded and out of action, three slightly wounded and hospitalized, and a dozen natives, men, women, and children who were passing by, lying inert on the pavement, bleeding to death. Nobody paid much attention to them at first.

The death of his son affected Jack Cobb severely. At first he couldn't bear to think about it. Then he began to talk to a few persons. With a handful of his intimates he wondered and speculated on where he had gone wrong. Perhaps he shouldn't have given Stanley the horse in the first place. The feeling of guilt that he entertained seemed to overwhelm him.

Then within a matter of weeks more bad news came: the failure of the Baltimore brokerage firm of Cobb and Stevenson. Overexpansion, a break in the stock market, and general business conditions were responsible. Jack Cobb had made a fortune and lost it. The big house at Cobb's Mill was on the market, as well as the stables and all the horses except Quicksilver.

Folks were positive he would spring back. Give him time, everyone said, and he'll be on top again. What they did not know was that since Stan's death he no longer had any interest in making money. His heart was elsewhere.

Jack Cobb's last night in the house was a warm summer evening. He sat alone smoking in the big living room, so empty and desolate now, so full of thoughts and memories for him. A house dismantled is a house forlorn. From a room in that house his wife had gone for good; in this same room he and Stanley had their last conversation and conflict before the boy was drafted. Each piece of furniture had been tagged, the bookshelves were empty, the books packed in cardboard boxes labeled for the public library.

The portrait of Dusty Miller over the fireplace was gone, leaving a faded oblong upon the wall. The cups and trophies had vanished, the home where Jack Cobb had lived so many years, gutted, the contents given away or made ready for the auction to be held the next day.

He glanced about the room, everything so meaningful to him, so full of memories of the past. Now he felt his life bent in two and was glad to be alone. Suddenly the telephone rang. Slowly and reluctantly he answered. His old friend Truxton Bingham, who lived down the road, wanted to run over.

Jack Cobb heard himself say mechanically, "Do come over, Trux. Be glad to see you."

Fifteen minutes later he heard the whirr of car wheels on the crushed stone driveway, the sound of brakes, and the slam of the door. Big Truxton bustled into the room, embracing Jack affectionately. He took a quick, sharp glance around the bare, empty room and fell into a chair, the same chair Stan had slumped in when confessing his "separation" from college.

How fast life moves at times, Jack Cobb thought. Several months before he had been a well-to-do broker with a son who was taking

28

honors at college and was the best young rider in Maryland. Now he was nobody.

Jack Cobb and Truxton Bingham were old friends. They had hunted together, raced together, brought up families side by side. They didn't need to say much, and for a while they sat smoking in silence. Finally Trux put out his cigarette and came to the point of his visit.

"Look, Jack, we've been talking things over in the firm, and we all want you to know there's a spot for you as a limited partner at our shop. That is, of course, if you'd care to come over."

Jack Cobb was moved by this offer in his time of trouble. Who wouldn't be? He passed his hand nervously over his forehead, showing his feelings. "I'm touched, Truxton, deeply touched. At a time like this it helps to have your confidence. Please thank the boys for me, but the fact is that for the moment, anyhow, I'm through with business."

His friend looked up quickly with a puzzled expression on his face. Jack Cobb retiring? He was only fifty-four; what would he live on? The horses and stable were to be auctioned off, but most of the money from the sale would be owed to the firm of Cobb and Stevenson.

"You mean you're retiring?" Truxton asked tentatively.

Jack managed a smile. "Not exactly. I've hardly saved enough from the wreck for that. No, I have a project in mind I haven't talked to anyone about, but I'd be grateful for your advice since you know the English racing so well. Briefly, Trux, I want to take Quicksilver to the Grand National."

His friend opened his mouth, then whistled. The mere thought staggered him. Truxton well understood the reasoning, for to win the National with Stan's horse would be a tribute to the boy. But the idea was impossible. Taking a horse to Aintree without plenty of money can't be done.

Jack Cobb broke in. "I know what you're thinking. To win the Maryland Hunt and the Grand National has only been done once before, hasn't it? Harry Morgan, back in . . . back in . . . '66, wasn't it?"

"Nope, '65 I think."

Cobb waved his hand. "I realize the difficulties, but nevertheless I intend to try. There won't be much money, because almost everything I own will go into paying the firm's debts."

"I quite appreciate that, and I wonder if you've considered everything, Jack. You realize you'll have to train the horse in England too? No matter how good a jumper he is, a horse accustomed to our rails and split fences is seldom much good over those brush and water jumps. I tell you they're rough."

"No need to tell me. I've seen them." Jack Cobb knew the whole idea sounded absurd and quixotic to his friend. "Point is, Trux, this was one of Stan's last wishes. Before the Maryland Hunt he talked about it."

"Oh, I see," said his friend. "I see. That does make a difference. Then you're determined, are you?"

"Absolutely. My idea is to stay the winter with some competent but little-known trainer, a man who runs a small stable and is willing to gamble a bit. In fact, it's all a gamble. I'd work out there through the winter and hope the trainer can find me a jockey."

His friend leaned forward. "A grand idea, but the odds are heavily against you, Jack."

"I realize that."

"You've no idea how the horse will take to English turf or the winter climate."

"I'm well aware of all you say. But Quicksilver is young, he has power, and if we can find a good rider, if he's well trained by a real trainer, his chance is as good as anyone's. The Grand National is a race full of luck."

"Then more power to you." A wild idea all right, but the more he thought about it the more it appealed to Truxton Bingham. "O.K., if you're set on this, I think maybe I know the man for you. He's a chap a bit over thirty-five, son of a top-class trainer, and he's starting out for himself with only a few horses. I met him last summer and visited his place on the South Downs. What was the name of that town? Stapleton, Stapleford? Something like that."

Jack Cobb instantly sat up straight. His face was animated for the first time that evening. "Be a good friend, Trux, write him for me, will you please? He sounds like just the sort of trainer I'm looking for."

Truxton shook his head. "I'll call him. That's far better. My first reaction was against the whole plan, but you've convinced me it's worth a try."

Then, promising to get in touch with the trainer the next day, he left, waving off Cobb's thanks.

"I'll see you tomorrow, Jack, as soon as I've talked to this man. Chester Robinson is his name."

Once again Jack was sitting alone in his dismantled living room.

4

He left the small train at a tiny station surrounded by rose boughs and flowers abloom. The train beep-beeped and moved on. He looked around. Nobody. Then a figure appeared at his elbow, hand extended.

"Good evening, sir. I'm Henderson, the head lad." That outstretched hand seemed to say, "I'm a good fellow, and so are you. Let's make the best of things."

Jack Cobb grasped the hand and reached down for his bags. The groom was quicker and got to them first. He seemed about fifty, spare, lean, with a tough, weatherbeaten face and the walk of a person who has spent much of his life on horseback. He wore a well-cut pair of jodhpurs, polished boots, a sports jacket with a shirt and necktie. On his head was an ancient derby with a wide brim, dating back forty years.

"Mr. Chester sends his regrets, sir. 'E has a client this evening to look over a gelding." And with that he led the way outside to a small parked car. An Austin, it was so tiny and the roof so low that the head groom had to remove his hat to sit at the wheel. Wedging Jack's two large bags into the rear seat was equally difficult. The car moved out, and they left the station yard and the village behind. The late afternoon sunshine was pleasant, the air warm and filled with the scents and smells of the countryside.

Although they were not on a main highway, Jack immediately noticed the traffic, a stream of trucks, small cars, and buses all going at about thirty miles an hour in single line. The next thing that attracted his attention were the gently sloping hills down to the sea in the distance. The Downs, so the groom announced. The car soon edged along narrow lanes, past thatch-roofed cottages, brick entrance gates to apparently large estates, and through little villages until at last after twenty minutes they came to a road bordered by high hedges. Turning into a lane only wide enough for one car, they twisted past a small cottage and came to a large, yellow-brick Victorian mansion. At the side was a stable with a dozen box stalls, the horses' heads protruding from each one. Before the house stood a young, tallish man talking to a couple, quite obviously clients. As the Austin rolled to a stop, the young man disengaged himself and came over to Jack Cobb, who was trying to get out of the car.

"Very nice to see you, sir. Welcome to the Hall. Sorry not to be able to meet you at the station, but these people phoned and came down rather unexpectedly. I shall be at your service shortly. Mrs. Robinson wants you to have a drink and dinner with us this evening. Henderson!"

"Yes, sir." Cobb could have sworn that the groom clicked to attention.

"Take Mr. Cobb and his bags over to Mrs. Briggs. That's where you'll be staying. Wait for him, Henderson, and bring him back here."

"Right, sir." They climbed back into the tiny Austin, and Cobb learned that Quicksilver had not arrived, but was due the next day directly from Heathrow Airport in London.

Henderson drew up beside a small brick cottage, half smothered in ivy, jumped from the seat behind the wheel, and, hauling the bags out, knocked on a highly polished brass knocker attached to the door.

"Mrs. Briggs! Mrs. Briggs! The gentleman from Emerica."

The door opened suddenly, so suddenly that someone could have been standing there and probably had been. A stoutish woman in a spotless white apron that covered her entire frontispiece stood there with a surprised look on her face. "My goodness, Mr. Henderson, you did give me a start. Have you been waiting long?"

She seemed flustered. Evidently expecting a red Indian in war paint, thought Jack Cobb.

"Come right in, sir. Come in, please. This way." Once inside she turned suddenly on him. "Have you had your tea yet? No? Ah, you won't be wanting any. Well. . . ." There was a note of regret in her tone as if to suggest that after all what could one expect from people who came from America? "It *is* a bit hot this afternoon." She threw open a door. "Now this is your quarters here. Nice and quiet with full morning sun. You'll be having your meals on that table there. *With* a private bath." She threw open a side door disclosing a toilet, a washbasin, and an ancient tin bathtub.

"I do hope this will be satisfactory." Her tone implied that if the accommodations were not, he was a fussy man, typically American.

As she paused in the flow of words, Jack Cobb intervened. "It's fine. What'll be the price of this, Mrs. Briggs?"

She responded quickly and without any hesitation. "Sir, the way prices do be going up, I shall have to charge you fourteen pounds a week. That's for the room, two meals, plus an extra one-and-six for the morning tea. You'll be wanting morning tea, I suppose?"

She glanced at him tentatively in a way that made Jack Cobb suspect she was overcharging him. He did a quick sum in his head. The whole thing came to about thirty-seven dollars a week, precisely what he had expected. The place was cheerless, with a grate about as large as a transistor radio, and he would surely be cold in winter. Still, there was no choice. He did not care to bargain, and he nodded.

She seemed relieved. "No doubt, sir, since you have a horse at the Hall, you'll ride out with Mr. Henderson each morning. What time will you be having your morning tea?"

At this point the head lad, who had been hovering in the rear, spoke up. "We try to push off for the first ride at seven thirty, sir, seven thirty sharp, that is. Better say a half after six, Mrs. Briggs. That'll give him plenty of time for dressing. He'll need his tea when we get that chilly winter wind off the sea."

Mrs. Briggs returned to the attack. "Daresay you'll ride and have your breakfast with the lads at the Hall afterward?"

Both men assented, and Henderson suggested that Jack join them on the first ride tomorrow even though Quicksilver had not arrived yet. Then he waited while Jack changed his clothes for dinner.

Later that evening, after an excellent meal with the hospitable Robinsons, Jack sat down in his quarters to go over his finances for about the tenth time within the fortnight. The room and meals would come to about a hundred and fifty a month. The cost of training Quicksilver was about the same per week, making a total of seven hundred and fifty dollars a month. Obviously things were precarious. His slender budget would not last more than six or seven months. The horse would simply have to win that year for his own survival. The odds, as Truxton Bingham had remarked that last, lonely evening in Jack's living room, were heavily against him.

When Mrs. Briggs knocked on the door the next morning with a lukewarm, muddy drink in a cup, he hastily swallowed it, dressed, and set out for the Hall. "The lanes are difficult the first time if you're not watchful, sir. First left, then by the thatched cottage. That'll be the Widow Stanleigh. Take the second right, you'll have a view of the water. Next right, and straight ahead for the Hall."

Unfortunately, Mrs. Briggs's directions were confusing, and he soon became lost. A man going past on a bicycle set him straight after he had mucked around for twenty minutes. At last came the view of the Channel, distant and misty through the trees in the morning sun. In a minute he made out the big yellow brick house. He strode on quickly, glanced at his watch, and discovered with some dismay that he was a few minutes late.

There, as he came around to the stables, stood the head lad in clean but worn jodhpurs, a sports coat with a necktie on, plus a cap instead of his derby. The horses were milling around, being mounted by the stable lads.

"Good morning, Mr. Cobb," said the head lad. "You're ten minutes late, sir. Now then, kindly mount that gray mare over there by the stable wall."

Confused, and a bit irritated by the groom's rebuke, Jack Cobb walked over, patted the horse's flank, shoved his left foot into the stirrups, and, helped by a stable lad who was holding the animal, got into the saddle. At the far end of the yard the horses were already walking around impatiently in single file. Cobb settled into the saddle, took the reins, clicked with his teeth, gave a sharp kick, and yanked the mare to the right.

Perhaps that tug on the bit and the sudden kick by a stranger were too much. Whatever the reason, the next minute he was on the ground, rolling over on the grass-covered cobblestones. His wind was completely knocked out. He could hardly breathe, and his right shoulder pained him acutely. Through the pain he could distinguish the subdued murmur of the stable lads. All heads were turned on him.

Furious with himself, with the lads, with the head groom, he stumbled to his feet, went up to the horse, put his foot in the iron, seized the reins, and, still panting from pain and annoyance, pulled himself into the saddle. As he fell into line and the procession moved toward the sea, the titters up ahead were audible.

5

The stableboys, or "the lads," as they were called around the Hall, greatly interested Jack Cobb. There were sixteen or seventeen of them, including the traveling head lad, who was in charge of the horses when they went off by motor horse box to race meetings. Each lad was responsible for two horses, riding out first one and then the other as they were exercised every morning on the Downs. The lads worked hard, starting at six thirty in the morning and ending perhaps at seven thirty in the evening. In between there was a long afternoon break, except when they went away to a distant race meeting.

Several girls were included in the group. They wore pants and windbreakers like the boys and had the same weather-beaten, horsey look. Every bit as effective and diligent as the boys, they were chiefly distinguishable by the fact that in bad weather they wore scarves tied around their heads.

Everyone at the Hall was friendly and co-operative, save one person. He was George Atherton, the contract jockey attached to the stable. When he met Cobb, he merely grunted and turned away. Chester Robinson explained that he had a bad ulcer. "It acts up on him sometimes, and one has to make allowances." This Cobb was quite willing to do.

Unlike some trainers, Chester Robinson owned several motor horse boxes for taking horses to race meetings. However, to meet Quicksilver at Heathrow, he had arranged with the Lambourn Horse Box Company to collect him. This company cleared him through customs for travel in the United Kingdom. It was late morning when Quicksilver arrived at the Hall, and a cluster of lads, including Robinson and the head lad, gathered to see the horse that had won the Maryland Hunt Cup and now hoped to run in the Grand National.

The box driver unlocked the door and let down the ramp. Inside was Quicksilver, trembling. He looked as though he had not traveled well, and Robinson and the head lad could not persuade him down for several minutes.

"He'll want water first off," said Chester, addressing a lad named Ginger with red hair, who was assigned to Jack Cobb. "Likely he's somewhat upset by the journey."

Quickly Ginger brought Quicksilver a pail of rainwater, which was the only kind the horses were permitted to drink at the Hall. After several minutes of walking him around, and some quiet affectionate words in a low tone from Cobb, the trembling ceased. Jack then led him to the stall prepared for him.

The trainer, on looking him over, suggested that they let him rest for the first day. "I can see the journey has worried him. In the morning he can go out with the first lot and have a couple of canters. We must go slow with him until he finds his legs and gets used to us. Basically, he seems to me to be in good shape. That's a grand horse you have there, Mr. Cobb. No doubt about it."

A driver from Lambourn's stood beside Cobb. He had a clipboard with numerous papers. "I wonder whether I can get your signature in quadruplicate on these receipts, sir?"

This done, Cobb left the stableboys, for the journey had taken a toll on him, too. Consequently, he turned in early, tired and anxious to be ready for the morning. Shortly after eleven that night there was a frantic pounding at the door outside, and then a brisk knock on his sitting-room door.

"Mr. Cobb, sir. Your stableboy wants to see you."

Stumbling to his feet in the dark, he followed Mrs. Briggs to the front door. There in the pitch blackness was Ginger Jones, leaning on his bike and panting.

"Your horse, sir. He's sick like and sweating. Doesn't look too well to me. I've notified Mr. Robinson, but you had better come around to the stables."

Hastily throwing on some clothes, Jack borrowed Mrs. Briggs's bike and tried to follow Ginger up lanes, down shortcuts and passageways, the whole way indistinct and uncertain in the darkness. The bike was old and wobbly, and he took several tumbles that shook him up. Finally they reached the stable yard, which was floodlit. People were moving around; the horses were jittery and pawing at the doors.

One glance at Quicksilver told him that the horse *was* sick. His head drooped, and he kept trying to lie down. Robinson with an electric torch in his hand was inspecting him carefully, feeling his stomach, which made Quicksilver shy away. One sick horse can send an epidemic through a stable and needs watching.

"He's not right—that's plain—and he has a temperature. So I called Doctor Sanders, the vet attached to the Hall. He's coming over in a few minutes."

As they spoke car headlights showed on the yellow brick walls of the house, flashing on the windows of the Hall. Then the lights of the car went out, a door slammed, and down the long corridor between the horses tramped a youngish, alert man with a torch in one hand and a black doctor's bag in the other. Good-evenings were exchanged all round.

"This is the horse, Doctor. Belongs to Mr.

Cobb here, and just arrived from Heathrow this afternoon."

The doctor nodded and said nothing but felt the horse's stomach as he tried to lie down. Then he looked in his mouth, took his temperature, felt his chest, and listened with a stethoscope carefully and competently. Obviously he knew his business.

Next he opened his bag, pulled out a bottle of pills, and with quick, deft movements stuffed two down the animal's throat. "My guess is that he caught a chill on the way over. Wait a minute. . . ."

Quicksilver tossed his head and tried to turn away from him. The doctor continued his inspection with the stethoscope. At last he declared, "Sorry to say your horse has a touch of colic."

"Colic?" answered Cobb. "Now how could he have gotten that? Just three days ago, when he left Maryland, he was in perfect shape."

The vet looked at him coldly. "Can't tell you, sir, but he has it now. Let's see . . . in four hours be sure he takes two of these." He handed an envelope over to Chester Robinson. "I'll look in first thing in the morning. Meanwhile, don't let him lie down. Keep him standing, better still walk him, lead him round no matter how exhausted he seems. If he doesn't get better, I'll give him some different medicine, but I'd like to see the colic pass naturally. Well, good night, gentlemen."

And he was off in his car, briskly bumping down the lane.

The two men and the stableboy looked at each other. "The boy and I will handle this, Mr. Cobb," said Chester Robinson. "We'll see him through the night between us."

Cobb looked up quickly. "That's kind and thoughtful, but he's my horse. This is up to me. Ginger and I will take turns walking him. How about that, Ginger?"

The boy agreed almost eagerly. One would have thought that walking a horse around all night was his idea of a good time. Reluctantly the trainer left for bed. The lights in the Hall went out, first on the ground floor, then on the second floor. Only the floodlight in the court remained.

"An hour on and an hour off. One hour is about as much as I want at one time, Ginger."

"Very good, sir. But Mr. Cobb, this is what I'm hired for, and perhaps I'm a little more used to it than you are. Why not ride back on the bike and get some sleep? I can hold out the rest of the night. It's getting on midnight now, and the vet will be back at seven. That's only seven hours."

"Thanks, my boy, but no. The horse is mine, and I should take the responsibility for him. Just pile up some clean straw for me in the corner of an empty stall, and then carry on while I rest. I'll spell you at one o'clock."

"Very good, sir. If he gives me any trouble, I'll notify you at once. Come on, old boy. . . ." Ginger led Quicksilver by the bridle onto the cobbled stones of the courtyard.

Jack Cobb lay down to rest. He could hear the tired *clop-clop* of Quicksilver's hooves, and, worried though he was, the sound seemed to put him to sleep. Next thing he knew, he woke up with a jerk. A dim light showed through the stable windows to the east across the Downs. Sleepily he looked at his watch. Almost five o'clock. That boy was still walking Quicksilver. Or had he given up?

Then he listened and heard the *clop-clop* of the hooves. But even to his sleepy ears there was a different cadence in the walk of the animal.

Evidently his stomach had relaxed after the several hours of tramping up and down the grass-grown cobblestones, and his stride was more normal. Cobb rose and went out.

Through the distant dawn he made out Ginger, feet dragging, stumbling round and round the cobblestones. He went over and took the bridle from the boy's hand.

"You shouldn't do that, sir. I'm all right, and your horse is coming along famously. I almost had to drag him at first."

"Good lad. Did you think to give him those pills the vet left?"

"Yes, sir. Took them like an angel, he did. Must have known they would help. I'll just turn him over to you for a few minutes." He handed the bridle to Cobb and walked toward the Hall, stumbling as he went.

6

Doctor Sanders knew his job. After three days'
rest, all signs of the colic vanished and Quicksilver was his perky self again. Nevertheless, the
doctor checked him each morning. In a week the
horse began to take normal exercise with the rest
of the string.

Everyone from Chester Robinson on down
liked Quicksilver. He gave no trouble, ate well
and regularly, and nothing seemed to bother him
as he gradually adapted to his new surroundings.
Standing with his neck stretched out over the

top of his stall, he watched with interest the movement in and around the yard, accepting apples from the two Robinson children, eyeing the comings and goings during the day, observing the stableboys at their daily soccer game. He seemed to fit into the life of the Hall perfectly.

For the place was alive, turbulent and bursting with characters of every kind. Jack Cobb heard some describe the Robinson stable as "a bit untidy," but he enjoyed the place, looking forward to the daily ride with the first lot in the sharp morning air on the Downs, the light changing with the weather and the time of day. The clatter and chatter of the stable lads as they went about their work greatly interested him. These boys were shrewd, their comments on horses and owners often succinct and telling. After the first week, they treated him with ease, and he felt he had their confidence.

Escorted by Ginger Jones and before long half the other stable lads at the Hall to the Horse and Hounds, the village pub, Jack learned a lot about the life of the neighborhood. He found that the nearby villages were known for special characteristics. Thus, Melton was famous as the cricket town and possessed a patch of grass carefully rolled and mowed in place of a village green. There everyone—men, women, boys, and girls—played cricket, and some went on to the county cricket team. Much Haddam was celebrated for its barmaid at the Crown, a rather blowsy blonde who explained the facts of life to the stableboys at the Hall in a most practical manner. Meon Valley was known for its footballers, who were rough and usually victorious; Kings Winn, located on a river, for its fishing as well as for its osier rods.

The stable lads, Jack discovered, were country boys who had earned far more working in the aircraft factory at Farnborough, but they all loved horses and liked to be around the stables. Every one was an excellent rider, and a few entered the point-to-points at Musbery, the next town, where there was a small hunt. All were clever poachers, able to shoe a horse, diagnose an animal's malady, or repair a saddle. They were invariably cheerful, usually whistling when mucking out the stables.

Before many days the job of riding Quicksilver was assumed by George Atherton. Atherton raced the various horses in the stable, and Robinson had first call on his services.

The work rides, seldom lasting more than forty-five minutes or an hour, were held twice daily and consisted of cantering, with occasional jumps, to get man and beast used to each other. Once or twice a week, when the weather was especially bad, there were longer sessions of roadwork. Robinson rode out each time, splitting the horses into groups depending on their condition and schedules. Thus one lot might sprint, another gallop, while a few worked over the hurdles.

By ten o'clock the telephone started ringing with long-distance calls, some from the Continent or even the States. At ten thirty Chester's two secretaries arrived, and from then until early evening he was on the phone continually. Cobb liked his easy and relaxed way of handling owners, stable lads, the head groom, and the salesmen and furnishers who seemed to be around every day.

In the mornings Jack watched George Atherton on the horse. They suited each other, and Cobb could see how Quicksilver enjoyed racing, head up, mane flowing. He was proud of the way Quicksilver responded, as Atherton went over some low hurdles and then galloped off into the mist over the Downs. Indeed, he was an animal to be proud of, strong, with sloping shoulders, full of poise and balance, in short a beautiful sight under his skillful rider. Jack Cobb was bothered, however, that the Robinsons had not given him a weekly bill for the work being done at the Hall.

Robinson's wife, Violet, worked as hard or harder than anyone. She was the one who kept the accounts, hired the lads, bought the forage, arranged food for visitors to the Hall, generally supervised the place, and did everything save write and telephone owners and track officials. Yet although he had been there nearly a month, Jack received no bill. To anyone used to American methods the friendly, casual procedure was unsettling.

As they went into the fifth week he spoke to the trainer. "Mr. Robinson, as you know, I haven't unlimited funds and need to watch things. Perhaps you'd arrange with your wife to tell me just how I stand at the end of the month."

The trainer took this request in his stride. "Oh yes, your bill, by all means. Violet tends to them, but with one thing or another she does get behind a bit at times. Sorry about that. I'll see you get your monthly statement tomorrow."

The next morning at breakfast Cobb observed

a large, square, brown envelope beside his plate. The kitchen at the Hall, a huge oblong room, faced due east and consequently was flooded with sunlight—when there was any. It had great rows of copper pots and pans hung on the wall opposite the table at which the stable lads sat, wolfing their meal. Two Purdy guns hung on brackets; there were a dozen sporting prints around the room. Jack sipped his coffee, made for him by Violet Robinson; although he drank the muddy Mississippi they called tea in the afternoon, he preferred coffee in the morning. He watched the tea being made. Great handfuls were tossed into a boiler kind of affair, which once emptied was filled with more boiling water again and again.

Cobb stuffed the envelope in his pocket and after breakfast walked down the lane to what Robinsons called his "digs." The bill seemed an imposing document. Everything he owed was detailed in a square, legible British handwriting. The fees of the vet were included, and there was an extra or two, such as rent for gallops on the Downs, plus his extra breakfasts at the Hall, plus the boarding fees for Quicksilver. The total amounted to about $650. He did some quick figuring. His money would not last forever, but it should carry into the spring and the National in April. Especially if he picked up some additional by winning a race or two.

A second thing that bothered Cobb was that, although Chester was easy and approachable, he seldom commented upon the horse. Cobb's life was centered now upon the animal, and he knew that Quicksilver had been over the fences hardly more than a dozen times since his arrival. True, the horse seemed fitter and had never looked better. Yet a doubt lingered in Cobb's mind.

Finally he consulted Robinson. "Tell me frankly how you feel the horse is getting on. Has he thoroughly recovered from that bout of colic?"

They were in the living room of the Hall. Chester lit a cigarette and tossed the match into the big fireplace. His legs wide apart, he stood facing Jack, who sat in a large chair.

"Very happy you asked the question. The fact is, I'm pleased with your horse's condition. You may feel we don't push the stock here. We don't. I always felt that my father worked his racers so hard that they left too much behind and did badly in competition. I train on the theory that a horse needs stamina to race, and I go light on training.

No doubt you're amazed we don't give your horse more jumping?"

He's reading my mind, thought Jack. "Why, yes, I'm a little surprised."

"I quite understand, but there's a reason. Quicksilver has been properly trained to jump, and it shows. He doesn't need a lot of schooling. He just has to get used to our English fences. Is that clear?"

It was. Meanwhile, the horse took to the twice-a-day work ride, to English oats, and to the unusual spell of sunny weather along the coast. Then one morning Robinson surprised Cobb by declaring that he was entering Quicksilver at a small race at Windsor the next week, stating that he needed a good workout over English hurdles. The news astonished Cobb. Was the horse ready for racing? Had the vet been consulted? At any rate, the decision was up to the trainer, so Jack rode along to Windsor the next week with Atherton and Robinson in the latter's new Rover V8, 3500.

After some careful thought, Cobb decided to speak to Atherton about Quicksilver. "I imagine you'll find as we did at home that you'll do better to give him a long rein." He tried hard to be casual. "I always used to impress on my son that you cannot get good results from this horse by kicking him or using the whip much."

"Exactly," replied the jockey quickly. "I found that out one of the first times I galloped him. Gave a mere flick of the whip, and he seemed to sulk off. I'll remember that."

Jack knew that Windsor was far from the best English racecourse; however, he was unprepared for the lack of amenities. The stands were small and rickety, and much of the course could not be seen from the finish. In the valley of the Thames, it was low and apt to be flooded in wet weather. The day was drizzly and damp, and Jack wondered whether Robinson was wise to let Quicksilver compete under such conditions. However, the two other men took the conditions with unconcern, so Jack said nothing. The crowd seemed sparse, the field poor. Atherton didn't appear to press the horse, yet he soon had a two-length lead and was going well.

Then disaster struck. The field dipped on the far side of the course, and when they came in sight again Quicksilver was last. When Atherton slowly brought him back to the unsaddling enclosure, he was lame. Jack was horrified to learn that Quicksilver had hit a fence.

The course vet felt the animal's leg and diagnosed a bowed tendon. A somber group surrounded Quicksilver. Jack was in utter despair. They turned, watching ruefully as the stable lad led Quicksilver away.

The next afternoon Jack, with Robinson and the head lad, stood beside the horse. Gloom was spread over each face. Doc Sanders, the vet, felt the damaged foreleg, conducting X rays in his head. The twisted plate that had shod the injured leg lay in the exact shape of a figure eight on the ground.

A dozen fearful thoughts ran through Jack's mind. I should have questioned his running so soon. The accident is all my fault. Will Quicksilver have to be rested until it's too late to qualify him for spring racing? Half a dozen fears jammed his mind. Jack waited for the vet to rise and announce his diagnosis.

"What I'm afraid of is a bad sprain of the digital flexor tendon of that foreleg. Mr. Cobb, sir, there's only one remedy. He'll have to be fired."

No, never, thought Cobb immediately! Once he had seen a horse fired, and he never forgot it. To fire a horse necessitates putting red-hot irons around the injured tendon. The experience is barbarously cruel and painful for an animal.

The vet clapped his hat on his head. "True, it doesn't always work, but this is my professional advice for a bowed tendon. Should you care to call in another vet, by all means do so. Talk things over with Mr. Robinson here, and make up your mind. In the meantime, good afternoon, gentlemen."

Waving to the group, his black bag in one hand, he got into his car and was off down the lane with a roar.

Without further comment, Robinson motioned to the stableboy to take the horse to the stall and went inside to answer a telephone call. Jack Cobb remained in agony. To fire Stan's horse seemed out of the question. Moreover, such a treatment meant keeping Quicksilver from racing all winter. It meant utter and complete failure. Cobb stood there, sick at the mere thought of what lay ahead.

At last Robinson returned and spoke to him. "You know, he must have hit that fence very hard, but if I ran him too soon, I take full blame."

"Very good of you to say that, Mr. Robinson," replied Cobb. "Anyhow the fact is I'm not about to have my son's horse fired, no matter what."

"Don't blame you a bit." A flicker in Robinson's

eyes showed that he was thinking of the horse's background and what he meant to Cobb. "But what are we to do then?"

He reached down to feel the tendon again. Jack watched Quicksilver edge away, and his heart sank. The cruelty of firing ruled the treatment out, but also he rarely found it effective. Yet what then? Where could he find the money to keep the horse in England for another winter? He had gambled and lost. There he stood, stubborn and sick inside, a frown over his handsome features as he looked at the horse. "At home the vets don't hold much with firing these days. Surely there must be something else we can try."

Cobb's agony was visible for everyone to see. What had begun with such hope and high emotion, what started as a successful journey, seemed fated to end badly. He felt desolate and alone in this strange land, with the horse he loved gone lame at a critical moment. So disturbed was he, he could eat no dinner or even talk at the table that night.

Later Chester Robinson returned to the problem uppermost in their minds. "Fundamentally I agree that searing the leg of a horse can't help but damage the tissue, no matter what our vet claims. Most horses come out of this treatment with their speed reduced. That's always been my experience."

Jack nodded.

Robinson went on. "I do have one suggestion. There's a most knowledgeable woman up in Somerset who's done considerable riding and knows horses. She has taken two of mine with bowed tendons and nursed them back to health with physiotherapy."

The proposal seemed ridiculous. "What the hell is physiotherapy on a horse?" Jack Cobb asked scornfully.

Violet Robinson shifted uneasily in her chair beside the fire. The head groom, who had come in for his evening orders, stood there, cap in hand, plainly uncomfortable. Yet Chester Robinson never showed any emotion. This man, he seemed to realize, has lost his only son in a monstrous war, and now he is losing his last contact with the boy.

The voice of the trainer was low and steady as he replied. "I'm not quite sure, myself, really. Massage, exercise, things of that kind. Anyway this sort of injury is her speciality, and she has had good results. If only we could get her down here to see the animal, she might agree to take him and see what she could accomplish."

Hope rose, sudden and soothing, inside Jack Cobb. After all, he thought quickly, a football player who has a sore arm or leg gets relief from the soreness by means of a whirlpool bath and exercise. "All right. See if you can arrange to have her come down and look at my horse, please."

Chester Robinson pulled his long frame out of the easy chair and slowly went to his office to phone. The head groom stood silent and waiting. The room remained quiet save for the *click-click* of knitting needles as they flashed in the agile hands of Violet Robinson. After what seemed an age, Chester returned. His face was smiling.

"I explained the situation to her in detail. Mind you, she didn't say she'd take the horse, but she's as set against firing him as you are, Mr. Cobb. She'll be down for lunch on Friday, and perhaps she might be able to bring him round."

"How can I ever thank you, Mr. Robinson?"

"Don't try. I'm as interested in that horse as anyone. Let's wait until Friday, and see how she responds. Her name? Mrs. Hunting. Her husband was killed in the last war."

7

Jack Cobb had seen enough horsey English-women to fear the worst. Usually they were tall and ungainly or short and square. Friday noon, however, he was pleasantly surprised.

An ancient Austin, whose fenders told their own story, rattled noisily into the courtyard. The head groom, standing there and watching the stableboys about their chores, astonished Jack by his attitude. As a rule, he had the reserve of a sergeant major and seldom seemed impressed by anyone. That day he could not have been more deferential to royalty. He opened the car door and stood at attention as a woman stepped from the driver's seat. She was tall, with graying hair, and wore a tweed skirt and yellow sweater.

Taking one look at Jack, she held out her hand. "Ah, you'll be the American owner whose horse is in trouble," she said, shaking hands and looking him over attentively but impersonally.

Then as Chester Robinson, hearing that the car had arrived, stepped from the office and came toward them she greeted him with evident pleasure. Plainly they respected each other, which gave Jack some confidence, although he was determined to reserve judgment. A few banalities followed. Really fine weather this autumn. Most unusual. Yes, roads are crowded these days. Then immediately she shut off conversation and asked to see the horse.

Once in the stall she exclaimed, with an appearance of spontaneity, "My, what a magnificent horse. Criminal to subject him to firing. Here, just let me feel that foreleg." Jack Cobb felt impressed by the deft way she removed the ace bandage and even more by the gentleness with which her fingers moved up and down the injured leg. Quicksilver edged away uneasily. She patted him a moment and stepped from the box.

"Fire that leg, and the elasticity will be gone forever."

Jack agreed. "Yes, but what kind of treatment do you recommend for an injury of this sort?"

She turned and looked him in the eyes. "What sort of treatment? How can I tell until I've studied the X rays and done some work on him?" She smiled warmly and agreeably. When she smiled, she showed the best set of teeth in all England. And when she talked seriously about horses she half closed her eyes, as though she was thinking over what he had said.

Jack liked her approach and found himself slowly melting. Then he asserted himself. Hold on now, he thought, I'm giving Stan's horse over to a strange woman in a kind of desperate venture. He glanced at the others: Chester in his business clothes, the head groom in a checked shirt, necktie, and riding breeches. They all were hanging on her words.

"This is a special horse," he started to say. "You see, Mrs. Hunting, this horse belonged to. . . ."

She broke in. "I know. Chester told me about your horse over the telephone. I'd like to be of

71

use to you, Mr. Cobb, if I can. First thing is to get the horse's confidence, to show that the treatment he is receiving is doing his leg good. This takes time. Then I start by using compresses to draw out the inflammation. Next I give him a massage on that foreleg—oh, very, very gently at first—probably every two hours."

"Every two hours!" Cobb exclaimed.

"Exactly, if the X rays show what I think they will. Then I'd walk him half an hour to forty minutes, two or three times daily, at his own pace. Say as far as to that stone wall there. As he grows better and the leg strengthens, perhaps as far as the end of the garden." She looked around the circle of men, flashing that smile again.

Jack began to relax. Perhaps she can cure Quicksilver, and in time. She quite obviously knows her stuff. And yet . . . and yet. I'm taking a terrible risk with Stanley's horse. How long will the cure last? How much will it cost? A dozen fears and doubts flooded his mind. She went on talking.

"Now take your head groom here. Mr. Henderson, how many horses have you? Sometimes ten, sometimes more?"

"Quite right, Mrs. Hunting. Quite right." He

seemed to throw an accusatory glance at the trainer. Or was it Jack's imagination?

"There! You see. He simply has no time for intensive treatment of the kind I've described."

Undoubtedly a competent woman, thought Jack. Half listening to her talk, he saw Stanley that afternoon at the Maryland Hunt, with the red sash across his silks, at the last hurdle. Also what followed. Does she understand what the horse means to me?

At this point the groom was called away to the stalls, and Chester Robinson led them into his office. The two secretaries had gone to lunch, and they sat down.

Mrs. Hunting turned directly toward Jack. "Mr. Cobb, year before last I had a mare in far worse shape than your horse. Chester here rang up and asked me to have a go at the horse, which was to be thrown on the heap. After four or five months of treatment, she recovered completely, came back, and actually won eighteen races. Was second in the Cheltenham Gold Cup."

Four or five months would mean that Quicksilver can't race this spring, thought Cobb. He was in anguish. Could he afford this treatment for the horse?

"One condition," Mrs. Hunting added. "So

long as he's in my stable, he's mine to work with and do my best for. He's my horse. Then, whenever he gets fit and well again, I return him to you." She hesitated and looked over at Robinson, behind an untidy desk. "That's how we handle things, right, Chester?"

"Quite correct, Mrs. Hunting. That's always been our understanding."

Strange idea, thought Cobb. Shall I permit this woman to take him and try to cure him? Shall I turn him over to her completely as she suggests? He didn't care for this stipulation at all. But if not, what?

Chester was called outside, and Cobb seized the moment. He heard a strange, dry, subdued voice ask, "But how much shall I owe you at the end of the treatment?"

Her eyebrows raised. She pulled out a package of cigarettes and lit one. "Why just the usual boarding fees you pay Mr. Robinson and a fee of fifty pounds for myself. If the treatment is not successful, you pay nothing. As soon as he's well, back your horse comes to these stables. Since he's only seven years old, my guess is he'll respond to treatment fairly soon. Of course, one never knows. But you understand, as soon as he reaches my stable, he's my horse. I suggest to owners they think it over for a few days. You can talk with Chester and make your decision. Does that sound sensible, Mr. Cobb?"

Again he heard that dry, weak voice agreeing.

Then one of the secretaries entered. "Mrs. Robinson would be glad if you'd care for a glass of sherry before lunch? She's in the big room."

They went out together, Jack somewhat mournfully. The decision was one he did not care to make.

Mrs. Hunting, seeing his reserve, kept talking. "You know, he's a gorgeous animal, that horse. A kind of saucy boy, he is. I'd like to see what could be done for him. . . ."

Jack didn't smile. He never had heard a seven-year-old horse called a saucy boy before and was not sure he liked the term. Yet, as he reflected, it suited Quicksilver exactly.

8

The wind, brisk with the feel of winter, whistled off the sea, banging the stable doors and bending the trees far over as the first lot came cantering in from the ride along the Downs. The file swung up the lane, the lads blue with cold, and into the yard.

Jack, standing on the steps beside Chester, was upset and showed how he felt. "No news in the morning post? That's strange, isn't it? Don't you think it's odd not to have some word yet? It's been ten days or so."

Chester took exception immediately. "Personally, I find that an excellent sign. Had there been any bad news for you, we'd most certainly have heard right away. She wouldn't waste time on a horse that made no progress."

And yet. Chester had urged him to continue to stay with Mrs. Briggs down the lane during Quicksilver's absence, because her place was cheaper than a room in the village, and infinitely more so than in any city such as London. Besides, Cobb was a man conditioned to the countryside and horses, to the smell and sound of animals around him. Why should he change?

But the next evening he was discouraged again as he sat alone in his cheerless room lighted by a bulb too small to read by, decorated with a Black and White Whisky calendar and a framed color portrait of the Queen Mother on the wall. Fact is, he reflected, I'm gambling on that woman to rescue Stan's horse from real trouble. Doubts choked him. He missed the animal. There were moments when he felt he hardly could endure another day without him. Here we are, he thought, both of us alone and adrift in a foreign land, and in the hands of total strangers. Nice people, but strangers. Damn it all, I was weak.

I should have stepped in and told Chester I felt the horse wasn't ready to race. I lost everything through stupidity and indecision.

The realization suddenly came over him that he had become a vastly different person in six months. A year ago he was a prominent broker, president of his own firm. It was: Yes, Mr. Cobb. No, Mr. Cobb. He was John Insley Balir Cobb, a master of the Bexley Hunt, a director of the National Hunts Association. In short, the world was at his feet. Now everything except Quicksilver had vanished: his wife, his son, money, prestige, position.

Well, somehow, I have to hang in there. This is Stan's horse with which he won the Maryland Hunt Cup. I must know how the horse is reacting. Everything depends on it. This uncertainty is killing.

Days passed. Two more weeks went by without word from Mrs. Hunting. To be sure, Jack enjoyed the work rides and coming back to breakfast with the stable hands, always lively and entertaining. Finally, weeks after Quicksilver had left, he spoke to Chester again.

"Frankly, I'm worried. No news is sometimes bad news. Folks hate to send you bad news."

"Not that woman," Chester responded quickly. "She's busy, very, very busy, you know. She has other horses, and my experience is she seldom has time to communicate." He hesitated. "As a rule, she waits until an animal is completely cured and fit for racing again before she gets in touch with the owner."

"Still, I'm anxious about the horse. Do you think I could ring her up?"

"I see no reason why not. Try her after dinner."

Jack called that evening. The only available telephone was in Chester's office, and the call had to be made between incoming ones. When he finally reached the number, the voice at the other end asked who was calling.

"Mr. Jack Cobb, staying with Chester Robinson in Sussex."

"Ah, Mr. Cobb? You'll be calling about your horse, I expect. I'll put Mrs. Hunting right on."

In a minute her strong, resonant tone echoed in his ear. "Hello there, Mr. Cobb. How are you?"

"Very well, Mrs. Hunting. I called to inquire about your horse, Quicksilver."

After a hesitant second her answer was clear and agreeably pleasant. "Thanks for ringing me up. I should have been the one to get in touch with you."

Yes, correct, thought Jack, relieved and slightly annoyed at the same time. But how *is* the horse? Call it yours, call it mine, call it anything you like, but how is he doing?

"Frankly, Quicksilver didn't take hold at first. But lately he's been responding to treatment much as I'd hoped. The inflammation has subsided; in fact, it's pretty well disappeared. Best of all, the lameness has gone. But I do want you to look at him. Why not borrow one of Chester's cars and run over. Come for lunch someday."

His spirits rose. "I'd like that," he responded quickly. "Today is Tuesday. How about next Friday?"

"Friday would suit me perfectly."

Jack then asked directions to her place in Somerset. The route sounded complicated. How far was it and how long did she think the trip would take?

She laughed. "With our crowded roads, you'll need at least three hours for the hundred-odd miles. That is, if you don't get lost."

He did. What with the hours spent worrying about the horse and what he would find, about being late for lunch, the trip seemed eternal. At last he reached Shepton Mallet where she lived and stopped at the small post office. There he was told to go on three miles and take the dirt road to the right. Immediately he found himself in rich farming country, with cultivated land on each side, until he came to the end where a farmhouse in front of a large stable appeared. It was very low key and unpretentious. Jack stopped the car, got out, and knocked. A long delay. At last a blowsy female in an apron far from clean came to the door, with a rather hostile expression.

"Mrs. Hunting?"

Her face showed no emotion. She wiped her hands on the apron and opened the door. "You'll be Mr. Cobb? She's been out with the horses and hasn't changed yet."

However, she held the door open, if a trifle reluctantly, and led him into a living room with ceiling beams and an enormous brick fireplace, which had rows of horseshoes on each side. They were familiar to Jack: prizes won at various horse shows. Rosettes and ribbons decorated each one.

The woman stood there expectantly, still fingering the dismal apron. "Shall you be wanting something, sir?" she finally asked.

"No, thank you," Jack said, at which without a word, she turned and vanished.

He looked around. On the shelves and tables

were silver-framed photographs of horses. Still others were of a young jockey standing beside his mount and an Army officer in uniform. Engraved on the bottom of the frame was the date: June 6, 1944. The husband, killed in the Normandy landing.

He glanced around the room. It was not exactly threadbare, but nearly so. The seat of an armchair sagged, broken springs doubtlessly; the cretonne looked faded. The carpet beside the door was worn. One of the beams, certainly as old as the house, was cracking and badly needed attention. At this point his inspection was interrupted by a large, shaggy, ancient dog, who stumbled rather than walked into the room. An Airedale, he gave one short whoof at the stranger, wagging his tail rapidly all the time. He came over to be petted, and then with a heavy Airedale kind of grunt sank down and curled up before the armchair.

A sound made him turn. Mrs. Hunting came in, hand outstretched. He smiled uncertainly, reserved and slightly troubled. She paid no attention, but apologized for the delay and offered him sherry from a glass decanter. No sooner had she settled down than she jumped up with the impatience of an active person, walked across the room to a silver cigarette box, placed it on a small table near her, took a cigarette, and lighted it.

"Now then. You wanted to know about my horse, Quicksilver."

He nodded. I didn't come all this way for the ride. Get on with it, he thought anxiously. How is he? A slight frown came over his forehead. All the while he had the same feeling of being inspected as on the day they first met at the Robinson stables.

"Oh, he's a darling. Never a spot of trouble. A bit tricky at first, but as soon as he saw the treatment was helping the leg, he was oh so sweet. Must have felt himself getting better day by day."

She made a quick, nervous gesture. "Let's see, he's been here almost two months now. Of course, we aren't out of the woods yet. But I do feel that someday before too long I shall phone you to say he is hunting fit and ask you to pick him up."

Her face beamed. Jack had to admit her smile was attractive. A weight lifted from him; he was happy again after weeks of worry. "It's a miracle. That's what it is," he said.

Instantly her whole expression changed. Her blue eyes became serious, and she answered him sharply. "Not at all. No miracle. Just patience and hard work. Lots of both." She leaned forward. "But I do feel it's an achievement for a horse to recover from a bowed tendon and get ready for the toughest steeplechase in this country."

A most unpleasant bell clanged in another room. "Ah," she said. "Lunch is ready. My son won't eat at noon. He's in training and very strict about his weight. Please come in."

The dining room had a sideboard with some silver on it; the table was round, large, and shining. In a corner of the room was a kind of hatch, evidently leading to the kitchen. A platter of food was shoved through; then it shut with a decided bang. Mrs. Hunting took the large plate on which stood a dismal-looking dish of shepherd's pie—minced meat covered with mashed potatoes—and brought it to the table.

"Beer?" He shook his head. "Some wine?" Again he refused.

"Ah, you're like me. Liquor at noon makes me sleepy by three o'clock."

Once more the little trap door opened. A harsh

voice from the kitchen asked, "I suppose you'll be having coffee, missis?"

"Yes," she said, annoyance in her tone.

Jack distracted her. "Tell me now. What did your treatment consist of?"

She became professional again. "First I try hard to do everything myself." She started eating. "If a stableboy walks the horse or rides him, he may undo all the good I've accomplished. So after the inflammation subsided, I exercised him twice a day. Either my son or I took him out regularly. No horse stays in my stable more than forty-two hours without exercise!" She made a decisive gesture with her hand.

Suddenly she turned toward him, earnestly looking him in the eye. "Really, you know, I do envy you. He's a gorgeous horse."

This remark gave Jack a lift, because he knew she meant it. Someone in England showed real appreciation of the horse.

Before Jack could answer, the trap snapped up and a tray of coffee appeared. Mrs. Hunting rose and took it. Jack jumped up too. Apparently they had reached the end of the meal. No vegetables, no sweet, nothing fancy. But then, he thought, I didn't make the trip for the food. He reached for the coffee tray, but with a quick gesture she got it first.

"No, I'll take it. This is old Lowestoft. Not even my son touches it. Let's have it in the living room."

The Airedale, waiting at the doorstep and evidently not permitted in the dining room, rose with some effort and followed along at her heels. Jack took his coffee and sat down.

They drank silently, and then she remarked, "Directly we've finished our coffee, we shall go out and let you have a look at him. I do hope you'll see a difference in his condition."

In a few minutes she led him out, followed by the Airedale on shaky legs. That wretched dog, falling to pieces, seemed to Jack to typify the whole establishment. Only the owner seemed to be on top of things.

For there was no question she knew her stuff. As she talked rapidly he listened with attention. They crossed a field beyond the barn, and she pointed out a pasture. "See that paddock there? A few weeks ago it was newly ploughed land, soft as peat moss. That's where I first exercised him, so that the action and reaction of his foot was rather like this."

She clenched her fist and moved it backward and forward several times. "Do you understand? This motion makes the hoof sink in the ground a little, and this articulates the foot and immediately reacts on the damaged tendon. Then, as the ground in that small paddock dried out, we moved to another field beyond the barn that was also soft and spongy. Before long the horse noticed the difference in his leg, and whenever I went into his stall he lifted up his foreleg for me to work on it. By the fifth week he was all fire and go."

She kept on talking, but he did not hear. Because there, coming toward him, was Quicksilver with—he suddenly thought—Stanley on his back.

Same age, same vibrant, youthful litheness, same shock of tawny hair, same insolent seat in the saddle, exactly the same as he sat there cantering easily toward them. It was Stanley, yet not quite Stanley either. Jack pulled himself together as the horse heard and recognized him, coming over quickly and nuzzling his head in his owner's arm.

Stroking that familiar mane, scratching the back of his ears as he always did, Jack realized how acutely he had missed the animal over these long, lonely weeks.

Mrs. Hunting was saying something. "My son, Anthony. Mr. Cobb, who owns Quicksilver."

The young man leaned down, hand extended. Jack grabbed it. A young, firm, strong hand, a hand used to horses and riding them in competition. Damn it, thought Jack, just like Stan's hand.

"Mr. Cobb, your horse is superb. It's a joy to be on him. He's a bold horse, a National horse. I can tell you, I envy the man who rides him."

9

While Iris Hunting left to go and change into riding clothes, the young man dismounted and led Quicksilver into the stable, followed by Jack. As he did so, a drizzle began, darkening the sky even though it was still early afternoon. Inside, the stable came as a surprise. One glance told Jack, a former stable owner himself, where the money had been spent: here, not on the house or the farm. Plain outside, the stable was, in fact, immaculate. Fresh paint glistened; the clean straw gave a bright look to everything. Despite the smell of ammonia in the air, the ventilation appeared excellent. A passageway of yellow brick led along the six boxes, of which four were occupied. Each box had a window divided into two parts, so the horse could observe the courtyard and the surroundings. Everything was at hand: feedboxes, forks, rakes, shovels, water buckets arranged carefully on hooks. Beyond, in the small tack room, the equipment along the walls was expensive and shining. Large *No Smoking* signs faced the visitor on every side. He wondered whether the owner obeyed them. Most likely not.

Tony Hunting led Quicksilver into his stall. Immediately the horse raised his foreleg, anticipating treatment.

The young man laughed. "See that. You have an intelligent animal. He likes his treatment." He gave the horse some water and tossed a day rug of wool over him.

Jack, curious, remarked, "Tell me. Who does all this? Who takes care of the horses?"

The young man, leaning over the horse, glanced up with a puzzled look. "Why, we do, Mother and I. She tends the sick or injured animals herself. Often I ride or walk them for her.

When I was at Cambridge I used to come back every weekend and work fourteen hours a day. At the time we had Gamage, the farmer below us, who came in a few hours each afternoon. Now, of course, we manage all right alone."

Jack shook his head slowly. He knew the work even a small stable such as this one demanded. The place showed organization, care, and much attention to detail, besides a concern and feeling for horses.

At this moment Iris Hunting appeared. The Airedale followed at her heels, entered the stall with her, and slumped in a corner, giving an audible grunt. She felt the horse's tendon, asked her son whether he had picked out his hoof that morning and how long he had been ridden.

"Half an hour? That's quite enough. I daren't risk riding him through that wet, heavy ground today. One slip and we're in trouble."

With a gesture she held up her hand to Tony, who handed her a tube of embrocation. Slowly at first, then more firmly, she rubbed it on the animal's tendon. Her son leaned against the wooden stall, arms outstretched, obviously admiring her. Good Lord, thought Jack, she surely knows what she's doing.

This treatment continued for twenty minutes. Then, leaving the stables to her son to muck out, she went outside with Jack, followed by the dog. The rain had turned to snow, the sky darkening further as they returned to the fire in the living room.

"He's with that horse all the time and won't let anyone else saddle him or take him into the paddock. He has a passion for him," she said.

"Isn't it early for snow in these parts?" he asked.

"Yes, but it's nearly December, you know." She walked over to the window and regarded the gloomy countryside stretching into the dimness, a wind howling from the northeast. A tea table was laid, with a large, dark china teapot and bread and butter, beside the fire. She sat down and poured.

He studied her face, almost for the first time. Rather grudgingly he admitted she was quite handsome. He was looking at her in a new way.

"See here, Mr. Cobb, you mustn't risk the roads tonight. The snow blows terribly in these parts, and the wind is rising. Why not phone up Chester, and tell him you'll stay the night? Tony will dig you up some pajamas."

He protested, but not persuasively. In fact, he was relieved not to have to buck the swirling storm on strange roads in the dark. Nor did he look forward to returning to the cheerless room at Mrs. Briggs's after enjoying the warmth and companionship of these people. The living room was shabby, the big chair had worn patches on the arms, but the atmosphere was friendly and agreeable.

Tony entered stamping his feet. The Airedale in the corner raised his head and thumped his tail twice. When Tony heard Jack was spending the night, he nodded approvingly and declared that a real storm was blowing up fast. After tea, he made several trips outside, returning each time with armfuls of logs for the fire, the only heat visible in the room.

Before long a bed was made up in an empty room upstairs, and Jack and Mrs. Hunting went off to get ready for dinner. He came down to a roaring fire, and soon Mrs. Hunting appeared. Now she was different, looking taller than before, wearing a blue knitted dress that set off her face. He began to realize at this point her considerable charm.

They had a drink and went in to dinner. At

the end of the room, the hatch clattered up; the hatch banged down. Plates with food were passed out, plain fare as at luncheon, for which no apologies were made. Roast beef with sprouts, beer, and the inevitable biscuits and cheese. Tony ate well, Jack less so. Returning to the living room, Mrs. Hunting slipped out to the kitchen and returned with a coffee tray containing some weak coffee. They certainly did not spend their money on fancy living. Then Tony excused himself, remarking that the time had come to muck out the stables.

For a few minutes they sat silently facing the fire. Mrs. Hunting seemed uncommunicative. Suddenly she opened up. "That boy of mine. Ever since he's been riding winners for the Greystone Stable, I can't seem to do anything with him."

"Should think you'd be pleased to see him win," Jack replied.

"Yes, I am. But you see he's just down from the university, and all he cares about is what horse he'll be riding at Sandown or Liverpool next month. Another stable picked him up last week, and now he has a regular panel of owners who swear by him and simply won't trust their horses to anyone else in a race. He even talks of becoming a gentleman jockey."

She tossed her head, scorn in her voice. "What kind of life is that? I wish so often that his father were alive." She sighed and shook her head. "You know, Mr. Cobb, he was such a thoughtful, helpful boy, but lately he's become so difficult I scarcely know what to do." She hesitated again. When she talked of horses in the stable, the words poured from her. Tonight she was slow and hesitant. The words ceased. There was a long silence.

There, before his eyes, this competent therapist suddenly became a typical mother, unsure and upset by a son coming into maturity. How strange, Jack thought, that he should travel three thousand miles to find a woman with the same problem as his own. The situation is like Stan's and mine all over. She has a living to earn, a stable to run, and now this boy is bursting off on his own and becoming a man. I wish I could tell her some things about sons at this age.

Suddenly Jack found himself saying, "You know, Mrs. Hunting, it happens I've been through much the same thing. As I told you my only son suddenly dropped out of college to work and train for the Maryland Hunt Cup, one of our principal steeplechases. The moment he left college, his Army deferment ended, so naturally he got drafted."

There was a pause. She rose nervously and poked the fire, which flamed up with a roar. "Yes, I know. Chester told me your story. Perhaps that's one reason I drove down to see your horse that day. In a queer way, it reminded me of Tony. He's ridden since he had a pony at eight, adores racing, which he does well. I really believe to ride in the National would be his idea of heaven. I keep telling him what a short life a jockey has, but he imagines he'll be young forever. Whatever shall I do about him?"

"I wish I knew," replied Jack. "My boy had his heart set on winning the Maryland Hunt and then bringing Quicksilver over for the National. We had a hell of an argument about it, one of our last talks together." He became silent. The remembrance of those days was still with him. For just a moment Stanley was sitting across the room, his face stubborn and implacable.

"I know. I admire you. It's wonderful that you haven't given up."

"What my experience tells me," he said, slowly and very gently, "is that what you want for your son isn't what he wants for himself."

She shrank from his words, and he saw the anguish in her face. She's having a hard time, he thought, and now a stranger is giving her advice.

"Look," he continued. "You brought your boy up as a horse lover. He loves horses and understands them and wants a life shaped around them. Would he be any happier working in London in the Westminster Bank than down here helping you with Quicksilver's damaged tendon? Would he?"

He stammered to a stop. She put her hands to her face. Beside the fire the Airedale caught her half sob, raised his head, saw her distress, slowly rose to his feet, and stumbled over to put his head in her lap. With one hand she caressed his shaggy, unkempt hair.

Jack sat without speaking. The woman, so voluble and confident around the stables, was quiet. "There are many worse things than being a top-class rider in England," he said.

She dropped her hands. "No, it isn't the riding I mind or even the racing. It's the terrible risks that he takes. Someday they won't come off. Of course, this is why owners want him. Bold riders win races—or kill themselves—in the end. It's such a dangerous profession, Mr. Cobb. I believe that in the past ten years two hundred horses have entered the National and only ten percent have finished."

There was another long silence. Finally Jack got up, stood before the fire, and remarked, "Yes, there's a risk. But young riders should take chances to win. That's the kind of horseman Tony is. I think he's to be admired."

The dog at her feet rose, tail wagging. The front door opened and banged shut. Then, shaking snow from his head and his boots, Tony Hunting entered the room.

"Good job you stayed with us, Mr. Cobb. The snow is thickening and starting to drift." He looked at his watch. "What time is it?" He leaned over and switched on the television. "They're interviewing Paddy Maguire on BBC 1. Do you mind if we listen?"

"Paddy Maguire? Isn't he the man who broke his spine some years ago in the National?" Mrs. Hunting's voice sounded frozen.

Tony nodded. "Bad luck, that," he remarked with the casualness of youth. Then the clatter and buzz of television broke in, and there before them they watched a thin, pale, tragic little man talking to an exceedingly cheerful interviewer.

". . . here's the ex-champion jockey, Paddy Maguire, as he and his wife look back with John

Stone. Despite his accident, Paddy still regards the Grand National as the greatest race in the world."

The face of the little man lit up. "Ah, but it is, though," he replied in an Irish accent. "A difficult course, full of traps and dangers, but it's a wonderful thing to be riding in the National."

Jack glanced across the room. The boy sat on a stiff chair, leaning forward, his elbows on his knees, oblivious to everything but the two men on the screen.

"Tell me, do you feel the race should continue in its present location at Liverpool?"

"Indeed and I do," answered the jockey crisply. "It must be at Aintree. Otherwise it just wouldn't be the National, now would it?"

At this remark Tony Hunting came out of his trance, sat back, and nodded vigorously.

The man in the wheelchair went on. "You see, it's the only place in the world you get jumps like those. It's a thrill even to think about them."

The announcer picked up on this response. "But surely it hasn't been much of a thrill lately, has it? You have four sons, don't you? Would you encourage any of them to become jockeys and ride in the National?"

The little man's chin came up as he seemed to

be thinking over the question. "I tell you very frankly, if they wanted to and were good enough, I'd not stop them. Believe I'd be pleased. Mind you, I'd feel a bit nervous when the race was on, but I think I'd be happy to have one of them a jockey."

The three sitting there watched the television intently as the camera shifted to a woman beside the wheelchair. She looked worn, weary, her stringy gray hair betraying the strain of the years through which she had lived.

"Now, Mrs. Maguire, as the mother of four boys, how do you feel about their racing?"

"Ah well, when you're married to a jockey, you pretty well know how things are. But this—" She cast a quick glance at her husband beside her in the wheelchair and stopped.

After a slight pause she went on. "The day of Paddy's accident I went to Aintree and stood as close to the rails as I could manage. Then a riderless horse went by. It was Number 16, Paddy's horse. Someone said, 'Oh, he's all right, missis.' But the ambulance passed, and I recognized his boots sticking out. . . ."

Mrs. Maguire could not continue. The remembrance of the day became too much.

Blandly the interviewer concluded the conversation. "That was Mrs. Paddy Maguire, whose husband rode Fire King at the 1952 Grand National and fell at the Canal Turn."

Being horsemen, they all knew the danger of racing, yet they were shocked by this tragedy.

Young Hunting leaned over and turned the set off. "Too bad," he said. "Care for a drink, Mr. Cobb?"

Outside the wind in a sudden burst whipped snow against the window.

10

As Christmas approached, drifting snow often choked the lanes, blowing into the corners beside the thatch-roofed cottages and making riding on the Downs difficult. They did a lot more road-work. The days followed each other, often with a thick mist covering the countryside. But as if to greet Quicksilver on the morning of his return from Mrs. Hunting, the day was bright and filled with a welcome sun.

Jack stood on the steps of the office beside Chester, surveying the scene in the courtyard.

He recalled the trainer saying that people in the village were eager to see the horse, but he had not really appreciated the impression Quicksilver had made until that morning. Besides some tradesmen, there were a dozen farmers from the vicinity interested in seeing for themselves the horse that had been cured of a bowed tendon. Directing the traffic was Mr. Henderson, the head groom, impeccable as ever in his clean jodhpurs, sports coat, cap, and necktie.

With a roar the horse van came up the lane, drew into the court, and stopped.

"Stand back there, lad, and you too, miss. Stand back now." Mr. Henderson, arms outstretched, stepped briskly forward, unhooked the ramp, and threw back the bolt of the van. There stood Quicksilver ready to descend. Voices could be heard as the groom led him down the ramp.

"Ah, now there's a horse. . . ."

"He's a horse, he is."

Chester stepped forward and felt his leg. "Never know he had a bad leg, would you?"

Mr. Henderson led him up and down the yard, shoving a wide-mouthed stable lad out of his way. "Look sharp, you blokes. This isn't just any horse, you know."

Jack Cobb was pleased as Quicksilver, feeling the cobbles underfoot, tossed his head and mane at the familiar sights and sounds. His delight in returning was obvious, and he walked up and down easily with that wonderful springy gait. Then he passed his owner and whinnied his pleasure as Jack stepped down to caress his head affectionately.

"Yes, a magnificent horse," said Chester at his side. "She's done a great job on that tendon, Mrs. Hunting has. Just isn't anyone like her."

At this point George Atherton rolled up in his car. Seeing the horse led by the head groom, he stopped short, jumped out impatiently, and went over, an anxious look on his face. Stopping the groom, he kneeled down to touch the precautionary bandage around the foreleg. "Feels perfect. Not a trace of the injury that I can detect."

That afternoon Chester merely permitted the groom to walk the horse up and down the lane for twenty minutes. But the next morning he was saddled, and Jack had the pleasure of seeing him under tack again. He was the picture of fitness, his quarters betraying the power of his frame. Jack on the gray mare watched attentively as Atherton, realizing that Quicksilver was taking a strong hold, gave him his head and let him stride along. Coming back to the stables, the jockey rode up beside Jack.

"Mr. Cobb, believe me, this horse is on good terms with himself, and he'll be racing fit before long. What we have to do is run him in two races before the Grand National weights come out in January, so he can be handicapped."

The following day Atherton was away, riding in the north of England, so Jack mounted Quicksilver in the first work ride. Being on him again was a joy. They walked, then cantered slowly down the lane to the Downs, something he scarcely had dared hope for several months previously. He rode along gaily, listening to the chatter and arguments of the stableboys around, all with an eye on his horse. Then he let him out for several hundred yards, feeling at the end that surge of power which had brought Stan to the front in the Maryland Hunt Cup. Yes, they were right, all of them. Now to prepare him for the National.

They rode back into the stable yard, and when the horses had been fed and watered, the sweat taken off, mouth and nose sponged, the stable lads left for breakfast and Jack found himself alone in the stall. Carefully he unwound the bandage over the tendon and lifted the foreleg, passing one hand gently over it to see whether, after exercise, there appeared to be any soreness or sensitivity. He worked over it several minutes. The animal remained quiet. No pain, no soreness left. The tendon was healthy again.

He left the box, shutting the door carefully. That's it, he thought. Now for the National. What a damn lucky man I am.

As soon as possible Chester Robinson entered Quicksilver in a race at a place called Bognor. The horse ran away from the pack and won by four or five lengths, which brought Jack Cobb a purse of six hundred pounds. The next race was to be at Worcester.

The night before Jack sat in his digs alone. He wore heavy boots, flannel trousers, a thick pullover of Scottish wool, and a padded jacket used for riding. The British Isles were encased in bitter weather. Snow had fallen over Scotland and most of the Midlands.

On Jack's lap was a pad he used for his infrequent letters to Truxton Bingham. First, he rose and poured coal from an iron scuttle into the tiny grate at his feet. Then he settled back to bring his friend up to date on the events of the last five weeks.

After describing Quicksilver's treatment for the bowed tendon, Jack wrote, "The vet attached to the Hall feels that Mrs. Hunting is a bit of a crank because her methods differ from his. As of now, however, we seem to be standing well, and I still feel we have as much chance at the National as anyone."

Suddenly there came a loud clanging of the outside door knocker. Whenever he heard this sound he feared for his horse. Mrs. Briggs, moving about her kitchen, shuffled into the hall as the knocking continued.

"Yes . . . yes . . . I'm coming," she muttered, opening the front door. Someone entered, stamping his feet. Next came a few brisk words, followed by a sharp knock on his door.

"Mr. Cobb, sir. Your stable lad wants you."

Alarmed, because he knew there were colds running through the stables, he jumped up and threw open the door. There stood Ginger, his stable lad, swathed in an enormous muffler of wool, his ears pink with cold.

"Good evening, sir. Mr. Robinson's compliments, and he's just heard the Worcester races have been cancelled. Ground too hard for racing."

Jack, disturbed, yet relieved, gave him half a crown. After the door closed, he listened to the sound of Ginger's ancient bike clanking down the lane in the sharp evening air.

"No Worcester. Ground too hard," he scribbled at the bottom of his letter to Bingham. He had no heart for details.

11

Eventually Quicksilver was handicapped for the Grand National, and Robinson continued to enter him in preparatory races whenever the timing was right. Toward the end of February, Chester Robinson, George Atherton, and Jack Cobb went off to Sandown Park, a racetrack southeast of London. Quicksilver was giving away nine pounds, and some first-class horses were running in the three-mile race.

Here and there a crocus peeped through the soil, and Chester at the wheel of the Rover was

in the best of spirits. On the way up, Jack prof-
fered some remarks in general about horses.

"Horses, I've always found, want to please and
love attention. They thrive on routine and recog-
nize a person by sound, voice, or smell."

Atherton, however, didn't seem to be paying
the slightest attention, and Jack began to wonder
whether he had heard him. "Do you agree,
Atherton?"

Atherton, as though awakened from sleep, instantly aroused himself. "Yes, surely. When a
horse becomes sensitive to signals from one rider,
he will not respond equally well for another."

"That's just it," replied Jack. But he noticed
that Atherton lapsed back into silence again.

Shortly after lunch, at which Atherton ate only
a piece of toast and drank only a glass of milk,
he left for the jockeys' room to change. Jack and
Chester sauntered out to the small grandstand.
Beside the rail Jack immediately noticed Iris
Hunting in deep conversation with a tall, well-
dressed man.

"Jack!" He stopped. She never had used his
first name before. "Do come here a moment,
please," she said, moving toward him. "There's
someone I want you to meet." As he turned and

reached her side, she whispered, "Colonel Pomeroy, the racing correspondent of the *Times*. He writes under the name of Audax."

A distinct feeling of pleasure came over him as she took his arm and led him back. Her felt hat on one side of her head was smart, and she wore a new coat that also suited her. Jack tried to make conversation. "Your boy seems to have been doing very well for himself this past month."

She accepted his congratulations with a slight inclination of her head. "Not too badly, I feel. He's still as keen as ever. Colonel Pomeroy, this is Mr. Cobb, the American who owns Quicksilver, the horse we were talking about in the third. You'll like him. He's a quiet American."

The tall man in the Guard's overcoat and the derby held out his hand. "Howjado," he said. Jack found the extended hand rather limp, but the man was genial. "Likely horse you have there, Mr. Cobb. Saw him run a fine race. Where was it? Bognor, I think, last month."

Pleased despite himself, Jack smiled and replied, "I owe a great deal to Chester Robinson, and a lot more to Iris Hunting here. She brought the horse round after a bad tendon, and now he seems as good as ever."

The man nodded with enthusiasm. "She's unique, isn't she? If I may say so, you were extremely fortunate to have your horse fall into such good hands." He turned to Iris. "Is your boy riding this afternoon?"

"Yes, he's on a horse from Greystone Stables, rather an old mare who has speed but has never lived up to her possibilities."

"Ah, that must be the horse Tommy Wilson rode in the Irish National last year. Got into a mix-up at the first open ditch. Excuse me." Colonel Pomeroy turned away to speak to a man with field glasses over one shoulder.

Jack looked at Iris. Her eyebrows were raised, her lips tight. "A mix-up at the first open ditch," she said ironically. "Brought three horses down with him. Only the mare came out of it. One had to be put down that afternoon, another has never raced again, and a third is just used as a hack now."

"How terrible!"

She turned sharply on him. "Tony has every right to lead the life he wants. That was your advice, and it's still good. I must get used to it."

"Good for you," said Jack. An admirable woman, and a strong one.

There was no chance for more talk as people kept coming up to them. Cobb noted with pleasure and a tinge of pride that everyone to whom she introduced him gave that tiny flick of recognition as they realized who he was.

They moved nearer to the weighing room, and Atherton, dressed in Jack's silks with the red sash across his chest, came up briefly. He shook hands and mumbled something to Iris, then turned away as the starter called the riders over the loudspeaker.

"My word, that man looks bad. He must be in pain. Has a bad ulcer. He ought not to be riding today."

"Yes, I know," replied Jack, watching Atherton's stooped figure moving away. "He seemed unusually quiet on the way up." Ah, the English, he thought, always the stiff upper lip. The man was really ill. He turned to find Chester Robinson, but by this time the horses had appeared and were cantering up and down past the stands. They went to the starting post, and after the usual jockeying the field was off.

Quicksilver was carrying top weight in the three-mile race, and Jack felt the same sense of elation mixed with gripping apprehension that came over him every time he watched him begin a race and approach the first fence. This time the horses were over it all together. Before the fourth fence, however, two were moving out ahead, and one, he observed with delight, was Quicksilver. A head behind and pressing him—it couldn't be —was Tony Hunting on a small, lithe mare. In a few minutes they came around, Atherton still in the lead, Tony closer every minute.

Jack glanced over at Iris Hunting as the riders tore past the stands, then over the far fences. Her eyes never left the boy, as he went up and over, riding with grace and power, still struggling to gain on the leader. The crowd roared approval as the two entered the stretch. Atherton seemed in command, yet Tony was threatening every minute. They flashed across the finish in that order, the others several lengths behind. Jack, elated, walked over with Iris to lead his horse into the winner's circle.

A large crowd circled them, commenting on the winner and his possibilities. Atherton dismounted, handed over the reins to the stable lad, and left to change in the jockeys' room. Jack noticed he was holding his stomach.

There was a ripple of applause as Jack's name

echoed over the loudspeaker. He came toward the ring, leading the horse, and a minute later found Ginger Jones, his stable lad, at his elbow.

"Mr. Cobb, sir." Ginger was agitated. "You'd best come into the changing room. Mr. Atherton's that sick. They've called a doctor."

Jack felt sick himself. Atherton should never have been riding. He was a sick man! Why hadn't Chester noticed his condition? He himself should have stepped in and stopped the horse from running. Cobb remembered how silent and withdrawn Atherton had been all morning. Inside the dressing room a small circle stood about Atherton. His long legs were doubled up, and he was writhing in pain on the floor. A man, quite obviously the doctor, knelt beside him. The physician was injecting something into his arm. Atherton kept moaning, his pain plainly apparent.

The doctor looked up. "Who's with this gentleman?"

"I am," said Chester soberly. "We came from Sussex. Can he be moved tonight?"

"I shouldn't think so," replied the doctor. "He ought to be in a hospital. I understand he has an ulcer, and he's probably bleeding. In any event, he's far from a well man."

Atherton's valet, a rather ancient character who always showed up whenever he rode, came into the room. "The track ambulance is here, doctor," he said in his aged voice.

"Good. I can get him into the Weybridge Hospital, I think. Just let me go to the phone. If this is what I think it is, he'll be there at least a month."

Jack looked over at Chester across the dissolving circle, as the valet and two grooms came in with the ambulance stretcher. Neither spoke. Chester's head shook as he followed the stretcher, his concern plainly visible. This man, thought Jack, had risked his life by riding that day. How had he managed to stay on Quicksilver? He felt responsible. And now what? The Cheltenham Gold Cup loomed up ahead. Who was there to ride him? What would happen to Quicksilver at this crucial moment in the long, arduous journey to the National? First the horse, then the jockey.

At this moment Tony Hunting entered the room, wiping his sweat-stained forehead and standing aside as Atherton was carried out. He looked around the crowd of serious faces before him and came directly up to Jack Cobb.

"Mr. Cobb, that horse rides like a Bentley. I

know because I rode him daily for six weeks. If things go badly for Mr. Atherton and you find yourself in need of a jockey, I do wish you'd consider me. I'd give anything to have a go on him at Cheltenham."

12

There were five of them in the Robinsons' living room, all trying to decide on Quicksilver's jockey: Chester and Jack; Doctor Sanders, who as stable vet was taking part in the discussion; one of Chester's secretaries, a pleasant-looking English girl; and the head groom. The argument over who should ride Quicksilver at Cheltenham had become acute. Cobb wore a harried look. The head lad sat twisting his cap in his lap and turning it in his hands. Doctor Sanders seemed anxious that everyone realize how much he knew about horses. His black bag was beside him on the floor; atop it was his cloth hat.

"Suppose I just give him a ring to see whether he's available," Chester said.

The group had been conferring for over an hour and were no nearer a decision than they had been when they began. Chester left the room for several minutes and came back shaking his head. "Isn't free. He's promised to Sir Douglas McIntosh."

"Bad luck that."

"May I make a suggestion, sir?"

"Certainly, Henderson. Speak up."

"What about that lad, Rex Benway? I know Sanders thinks well of him."

"You couldn't do better, Mr. Cobb," interjected the vet. "'Course, he's a former stable lad—nothing swell about him—but I've found that he invariably comes through in a crisis. Known him now for some time. You might say I started him riding."

"I know Benway," said Chester. "Too inexperienced. But there's always this man Stevenson."

"Stevenson's free all right. Indeed yes, let out by Waverly Stable last month. He's got a rotten bad temper. Can't count on him."

"Ah, I didn't know that," responded Chester.

The vet appeared to know everyone in racing circles, and he had a reason that ruled out each man who was brought up except for his own protégé. Indeed, they could end up with nobody, Jack feared. All the best jockeys were either attached to various stables or had been booked by trainers. What a shame Atherton couldn't ride the horse, Jack reflected. They were in a desperate fix, and it was late to be choosey.

At last Cobb made a suggestion. "Well now, what about young Hunting?"

Distaste spread over the vet's face, and he answered with considerable scorn in his voice. "A boy of twenty-two, twenty-three? Entrust that great horse to a mere boy? Why, it's unthinkable."

"He happens to be twenty-six. My son won the most important steeplechase in the United States when he was twenty-two."

Sanders' upper lip curled ever so slightly. Plainly he considered a race at the Maryland Hunt Club in somewhat the same category as a race in Madagascar. "No comparison. What's this boy ever done? I saw him ride in Hampshire last autumn. Didn't like the way he handled his mount, not at all."

"How did he finish?" asked Jack quietly.

The vet paused a moment before he spoke, trying to be casual. "Don't remember. He placed, I believe. I'm not sure. But he wasn't impressive, not at all." Doctor Sanders refused to look at Jack. Quite evidently he felt his professional judgment was being challenged. Friction pervaded the room.

Chester in his good-natured way intervened. "Fact is, we haven't a great deal of choice at this late date. Why not state your reasons for picking young Hunting, Mr. Cobb?"

Jack immediately sat forward in his chair. "I will. First, we haven't many choices. Second, although Tony Hunting does lack racing experience, he's a bold rider. Third, Hunting rode Quicksilver every day while he was at their stable. They have a rapport that I feel is important."

At this point Sanders exploded. "A rapport! What on earth is that? Can he ride?"

Cobb took no notice of the vet, but continued to address himself to Chester. "This afternoon we've considered a dozen men, and for one reason or another none seemed suitable. Why not ask Atherton? He's ridden against young Hunting in a race. Can we talk to him on the phone in that hospital in Weybridge?"

"Yes, I was on to him yesterday."

Cobb sat back in his chair. "Good enough. Tell you what. I'll be governed by what he says. Suppose we try him and get his honest opinion."

Chester rose. "Very well, I'll call straight away." He left the room, trailed by his secretary.

The vet leaned over, picked up his cloth hat, which he clapped on his head, took up his black bag, and stood up. His expression plainly said that there was no doing anything with owners, especially American owners. Out loud, however, he remarked, "I really must be off. Due back at surgery in twenty minutes. Good afternoon, gentlemen. Good afternoon to you, Mr. Cobb, and the best of luck. You'll surely need it if you put up with that young man from Cambridge." With barely a nod around the room he was gone.

The head lad rose awkwardly, twisting his cap in his fingers and murmuring something about looking in at the stable. Then he, too, vanished.

It's come down to the end of the road, Jack thought. A tough decision, and all mine.

Violet Robinson entered with a tray set for tea. She hesitated and stood with the tray in her hands in the open doorway. "Why, Mr. Cobb, you're alone. Where's everyone gone? I've got tea for five."

Jack had to prod himself into replying. "Chester has gone to telephone Atherton. Miss Crane is with him. The head lad is off to the stable. The vet had to return to see clients. That leaves only me."

"Never mind," she said, coming into the room and setting down the tea tray. She pulled out a chair. "Have you picked out a jockey for your horse yet?"

He shook his head gloomily. "No," he said. "We haven't." He rose and took the extended cup. "Seems to come down to what jockey has the least against him. Personally, I rather lean toward Hunting, but the vet says he's too young."

"Mr. Cobb, you must be aware that Doctor Sanders is frightfully jealous. Don't let it bother you."

"Mrs. Robinson, I believe in the young. Those aren't just words either. My boy was racing at sixteen. If the young are solid, you can throw responsibility at them and they usually measure up to it. Think of those pilots years ago in the Battle of Britain, for instance."

"Yes," she replied crisply. "If it weren't for those young men, we wouldn't be sitting here now. I was a tiny girl at the time, but I remember. I also remember when Chester's father was ill. Chester was quite young then; he couldn't possibly run the stables. He didn't have any experience, he didn't know horses, and so on. We had some unpleasant moments, especially with an overdraft at the bank, and no way of meeting it. But he took over the place, he made mistakes and learned fast, and now we're solvent."

"That's exactly it." Jack paused for a moment. "I know this boy is not the best, but he's the best rider we can get today, the best one who is free. And I believe he's improving all the time. Y'know, Mrs. Robinson, he's a young man with something old in him. Feet on the ground all the time, like his mother. But I do wish I didn't have to make the decision myself."

"I quite understand." She smiled at him, and her blue eyes sparkled. "It's terrible for you, bringing that horse way over here and having all these things happen." She looked at him with sympathy.

Then he heard the office door bang, and Chester strode back into the living room. He looked around in surprise. "Where's everyone gone?" he asked.

Jack explained again. "Doctor Sanders had to get back to the surgery. Henderson packed up and returned to the stables. Chester, I hope I haven't caused any trouble with my suggestion."

Chester, in an unusual show of warmth, put his arm around him. "Not at all. Please believe me."

"Well, that's fine. Now what did Atherton say?"

"Says in a way we'd be lucky to get young Hunting. He thinks he'll do well at Cheltenham and perhaps in the National too. You remember at Sandown Park he hung on to the very end. Atherton was impressed."

"Seems to me," Cobb said, "that there's something about Mrs. Hunting that put off Doctor Sanders. Still I wish the choice wasn't up to me."

Unfortunately, the choice *was* up to him. At last, seeing no other alternative, Jack offered the job to Tony and asked him to come to the Hall. The boy arrived in his car late one evening about nine o'clock and was introduced to the head lad immediately. The next morning Henderson had him join the work ride with the stableboys, and the training started in earnest.

Tony rode Quicksilver exactly as the head lad told him and did well. He was always in control, and his understanding with the horse was perfect. During his time at the Hall, Tony was quiet and unassuming. Nor did he attempt to presume on his friendship with Cobb as he well might have done.

All were intent on one thing: the Cheltenham Gold Cup. They turned their gaze on this hurdle in their campaign to reach the National and kept it there.

13

Known as the National Hunts Festival, Cheltenham's March meeting was held about two weeks before the Grand National. Everyone agreed that it was one of the best steeplechasing tests and had the best entries, because many owners refused to risk their horses at Aintree on account of the toughness of the course and the height of the fences. At Cheltenham the famous Gold Cup, run on the last afternoon of the meeting, invariably attracted an immense crowd and brought together the best three-mile racers in the country, all carrying the same weight. The field seldom exceeded ten horses.

The week prior to the Gold Cup something hit Jack Cobb. He woke one morning feverish and dizzy, unable to dress, to walk across the room. In the evening he was worse, and the local doctor dropped in, called by Mrs. Robinson. A jolly, fat little man, he listened to Jack's chest and lungs, took his temperature, and whistled softly. He murmured that just about everyone in Sussex seemed to be down with it. What "it" was he did not explain, but gave Jack half a dozen pills and wrote out a prescription.

"This is Friday," croaked Jack. "Any chance of my getting to Cheltenham a week from tomorrow?"

The doctor responded quickly and briefly. "I shouldn't care to be responsible for you if you go. Most likely you won't feel up to it anyhow."

"Actually I have a horse running in the Gold Cup. Isn't there something you can give me so I won't have to miss it?"

The doctor sat up in his chair. "Of course! You're the Mr. Cobb who brought his horse over for the National. Folks in the village all say he has a good chance, too." He glanced curiously at the sick man as so many strangers did when discovering Jack was the owner of Quicksilver. "Ah, this is bad luck for you. Well, ordinarily I wouldn't permit you out of doors in this wretched March weather for at least ten days, but we'll check the end of the week and see."

Then he leaned over, shut his bag with a decisive snap, and rose. "How about that horse anyway? I hear in the village he's had a bad time since his arrival."

He moved toward the door and turned, his hand on the knob. "Mind you, if things get worse, just have Mrs. Robinson phone my surgery and leave a message. In any event, I'll see you before the end of the week. Good day, sir."

Out he went, leaving Jack alone and miserable. Bad luck that Quicksilver had had the colic, bad luck that he sprang a plate, bad luck Atherton's ulcer kicked up at that particular time, bad luck that he himself caught a flu bug. He turned over, staring at the wall, and soon fell into a doze. Then there was the sound of a car, and Chester and his wife were coming into the room.

"You need looking after, Mr. Cobb," said Violet Robinson. "We shan't allow you to be alone in this cheerless room." So, bundled in trousers and a sweater, his overcoat thrown over his shoulders, he left the faded calendar and the oleo of the Queen Mother on the wall, and soon he found himself in a huge bed in a large room on the second floor of the Hall.

In the evening Chester dropped by, and said, "You were quite right. The boy does know the horse, and what's more he handles him well. He's an excellent choice."

The next afternoon Tony, in tack, came to see him for a moment. He was quietly confident and the picture of health, full of praise for Chester. "You know, this man Robinson is impressive. I only wish I had another two or three weeks on the horse, but I'll do the best I can."

The trip to Cheltenham was, as the doctor had foreseen, far too much for Jack on Friday. Saturday turned out to be a fine, sunny afternoon, so, well wrapped in his bathrobe and blankets, he managed to navigate the stairs and hobble down to the living room, where he sank into an easy chair before the television set. The stable lads had a set of their own in the tack room, so Violet Robinson, Jack, the head groom, and the two Robinson children, a boy and a girl, were gathered about the fire.

The head groom spoke sparingly. "Mr. Cobb, sir, I've come to believe you've made a wise choice. I'm greatly pleased."

Jack felt happier than he had for a week. He well knew the imponderables against the boy, and the terrible importance of the race. It was Quicksilver's biggest and toughest test. Jack's fortune and indeed his future depended upon it as he watched—with all England—before the set in the living room of the Robinsons.

Anxiously Violet Robinson leaned over and switched on the set. The fresh greenery of the grass and the blue of the Cotswold sky now flashed across the screen. Then the commentator began to list the entries.

". . . are called Top Class, who as you'll remember finished fourth last year in the National; Davy, an Irish gelding ridden by the veteran Harvey Thomas and owned by Lord Beresford; George Beal, up on Steady Boy, owned by Sir Philip Hudson; the American horse, Quicksilver, owned by Mr. J.I.B. Cobb, who unfortunately is laid up with the flu and won't be here today. His jockey is Tony Hunting. Next is Pat O'Donovan, the Irish jockey, on Mr. Stephen Douglas's Champion's Choice, a real comer who has done some good things lately; a French horse called Pertinax, owned by Monsieur Marcel Dupont of Paris and ridden by Georges Bertrand; he is a seven-year-old, winner of several good races this past winter; and last of all, Rob Roy, owned by Mr. David MacDonald, ridden by . . . and here they come. . . . Now the horses are all out."

They were indeed. As they paraded in single file in front of the stands, Jack forgot everything, all his anxieties vanished as he recognized Tony Hunting with that red sash over his shoulder. He forgot his illness, forgot the many troubles of the winter campaign, forgot the long painful struggle, in fact forgot everything save his boy and his son's horse. If Tony does nothing today, if he takes a fall and doesn't finish, seeing that lad on the horse and the way he rides makes up for everything. It's Stan again, the same confident youth riding before the ripple of applause from the crowd.

". . . and now they're jogging back to the start of the three miles, two furlongs, and seventy-six yards of the Gold Cup, the forty-second running of this famous race. As you know, it is over a mile shorter than the National at Aintree, but as severe a test. A perfect day, ideal conditions, course in fine shape, and a big crowd. Remember, however, this is not a handicap race. All horses race at level weights. Now they're under starter's orders. Top Class a bit restless. The jockey takes a pull. Now Davy is out of line. The starter speaks to his rider. At last Davy is coming up . . . back in there. . . .

"They're off. . . ."

Once more Jack had to force himself to watch the horses take that first dangerous fence in a bunch. All of them made it safely. Then the field gradually spaced out, and Davy edged slightly ahead as they raced for the second, Quicksilver lost for a moment in the crowd.

"It's Davy first over the second hurdle, followed by Top Class. Champion's Choice by almost a length over Dancer's Pet. A longish run down to the third, the first three horses over, the others come along. Davy dropping back slightly here. . . ."

At this point Jack caught a glimpse of Quicksilver as the riders tore for the fourth fence. There was an open ditch that seemed to be troublesome.

Suddenly Henderson at his side exclaimed under his breath. "Ah, that's bad, that is. Pure inexperience."

The announcer caught the bobble also. "The American horse made a mistake there. He tried to take the fence a stride behind another horse and was very nearly on the floor. Now he's next to last, racing with Pertinax as they go down the hill. So now it's Davy, then Dancer's Pet, followed by Top Class, the leader running within himself, and a length and a half ahead. . . ."

"Look," Jack said to himself, "this is only the start. It isn't over yet." But his heart was heavy with fear as he watched Davy take the next fence superbly. Tony was riding confidently and well, not panicking, not pushing the horse or using the whip. No sir, it isn't over yet by any means. I've every confidence in the boy and the horse. . . .

". . . a great jump by Top Class there at the seventh, the stands applauding. He's keeping in touch and gaining on Davy. There . . . you can see them nearly level, taking fence after fence as they draw ahead at the halfway mark. Davy, a head over Top Class, three and a half lengths over Dancer's Pet, followed by Champion's Choice and Rob Roy almost together."

Never a word about Quicksilver, Jack thought. Look, this race isn't over yet. You don't know my horse. He's not out of it yet, not by any means. But inside Jack felt an aching doubt begin to grow, although he saw how easily Quicksilver was moving in the rear.

"Hasn't made his move yet, Quicksilver hasn't," murmured Mr. Henderson beside him. "Look there. There he goes now, sure enough. . . ."

Yes, he was. He was moving up, slowly, steadily. He passed Champion's Choice and Dancer's Pet, who was struggling in the rear, and gained. . . .

"Ah, there's a tumble," the announcer declared. "Top Class is down at the fourteenth. Quicksilver, the American horse, coming right after him, took off at the fence too soon, plunged through, and was very nearly a downer, too. But young Hunting managed to stay on, collected his horse, and they're off after the leaders. Davy first, then Pertinax, followed by Steady Boy, with Quicksilver fourth. Quicksilver is running strongly now. . . ."

"Go on, go on," shouted Violet Robinson.

"Mummy, he's gaining, he's gaining," both the young children shrieked together.

Henderson, however, was shaking his head. "Doubt if he can do it. Too near the finish."

"And a fine effort by the American horse, a wonderful jump at that last fence. He passed the Frenchman and is two . . . perhaps two and a half lengths behind. Can he do it? Look at that American horse! He's started to make a race of it. Too bad his jockey made that mistake, pure inexperience. Certainly he is gaining now, and the French horse is running too. He's right at Quicksilver's shoulder and is racing stride for stride with him.

"It's still Davy, with four to go. A beautiful jump by Quicksilver, who is perhaps one, maybe one and a half lengths back. He's not had a single bit of trouble since that disastrous fifth fence. Anyone's race. Quicksilver and Pertinax close together. So it's Davy inside . . . with Quicksilver pressing hard. They're over the last hurdle, and now that awful race uphill to the finish. Quicksilver is gaining, hardly more than a head separates them."

Jack Cobb buried his face in his hands. He and the head groom were silent, while the children and Violet Robinson shrieked as the horses neared the finish.

"Now Davy ahead slightly, Davy leading by a neck." The announcer was fairly screaming into the microphone at this point. "Davy goes across the line, the winner, I think, by the narrowest of margins over Quicksilver. What a race! Here come the others. Pertinax third, now Champion's Choice, and Steady Boy last. . . ."

A photo finish. An agonizing pause, as the judge waits to examine the pictures.

"So," the announcer intoned at last, "the Cheltenham Gold Cup results. . . . Davy, ridden by Harvey Thomas, owned by Lord Beresford, the winner by a head. Second, Quicksilver, the American horse, ridden by Tony Hunting and owned by J.I.B. Cobb, of the U.S.A. Third, Pertinax, ridden by Georges Bertrand and owned by Marcel Dupont of Paris. A truly magnificent race. I've never heard such a noise as the crowd made when cheering that gallant challenge of Quicksilver after he hit the fifth hurdle. There he goes, the crowd giving him a well-deserved ovation."

Then Chester came on the screen with a wide smile. In the room they all talked at once as the Gold Cup was presented to the winner, a tall Englishman in a bowler hat.

Suddenly the telephone in the office rang. Violet stepped out to answer it. "It's for you, Mr. Cobb," she said on her return.

Jack tossed aside the blanket and stumbled down the hall, weaving into Chester's office. Like the rest of him, his voice was weak and trembling.

"Mr. Cobb." Iris Hunting was speaking. "I had to call. Hope you weren't disappointed with the result."

"Not exactly, no indeed," said Jack, somewhat out of breath.

"Look, I always told you he was a National horse, didn't I?"

"You certainly did. Congratulate your boy for me. He was smashing. Tremendous when he hit that fence and came through."

"Can't get a good connection. Wish you were on hand here to lead him in."

"I wish so, too," Jack replied. He suddenly had a strange desire to sit down.

14

Jack, after a sleepless night, reached Aintree and walked out on the course. He was at the third fence, the first open ditch, not easy to get over. It was a barrier of thick spruce and brambles, impenetrable, through which no horse could bull his way. Jack was not an especially small man, yet this fence towered above him as he stood beside the ditch. He shook his head and stepped into the jockeys' room. It was still two hours before the men were called, but everyone was present, a milling throng.

Later that afternoon as Jack passed the official at the door and went inside again, he felt immediately the electricity among the riders. It was natural. Jockeys were sitting around in all stages of dress and undress, some of them nervously smoking, some lighting cigarettes and extinguishing them. Who will get back unscratched? That insignificant little chap may be all right, while the big fellow over there returns in an ambulance. On the National, all bets are small, because luck and chance play such an enormous part in victory or defeat.

For just a few seconds the lights from the high windows were blinding. Gradually Cobb was able to take in the scene. Some of the jockeys were sitting on benches, hands upon their knees, some were quietly talking or passing back and forth to the toilet, but nobody was laughing or joking. Presently Jack made Tony out, sitting quietly in one corner. An amateur among the pros, he must feel completely alone.

Perhaps a friendly face would do him good, and indeed he greeted Jack with evident pleasure. How had he slept?

"Dreadfully. Wretched night," he replied.

Jack, who hadn't slept much himself, turning

and tossing until the English dawn broke, well understood how he felt. "Cheer up. Once you get going you'll feel great."

"Perhaps. I certainly don't now."

Then suddenly the boy rose and, shoving Jack somewhat rudely out of the way, made for the toilets. He was gone for a long while, but when he returned seemed more himself.

"Please forgive me, Mr. Cobb. It must have been something I ate last night."

The explanation was a brave attempt at a joke, and Jack's heart went out to him. He knew just how the boy felt and tried his best to encourage him.

"Buck up, lad. We've got a good, sound horse. Nobody knows it better than you do. Remember, you might easily have won at Cheltenham but for that mistake at the fifth. You very nearly caught the leader going up the hill to the finish. The odds are coming down now. But Chester has told you all this. If you stay out of that scramble at the start, you'll come through. We only need a break to make a run for it."

Tony's light eyes rested on Cobb skeptically. "Very nice of you to say so, Mr. Cobb. I want to win, not do well. Of course, I'll do my very best.

Count on that. I certainly wouldn't swap my horse for any mount in the race."

His frame was slender like his mother's. He did not have an aggressive air, and he seemed quite incapable of competing in the rough race. But although he appeared too frail to overcome the buffeting of the track, Jack was confident.

"I'm positive you'll finish, Tony. I'm sure you will. Just remember not to make your bid too soon. You have a horse with strength and stamina. Let somebody else force the running. Here's Chester. He'll tell you the same thing. Well, I'll leave you two alone, and I just wish you all the luck in the world, son."

He took Tony's outstretched hand. It was icy, but the grip was firm and determined. Jack knew enough about racing to realize that running on an empty stomach could be helpful.

"Thanks lots, Mr. Cobb. Believe me, your confidence helps me. And thanks for giving me this chance."

Cobb left the trainer alone with the boy and turned to go. Waiting just outside the weighing room was Iris Hunting. She was the mother now.

"I knew you'd be in the jockeys' room. How is he?" she asked.

"Naturally he's edgy," he said, deciding not to mention the throwing up.

"He has every right to be so," said Iris.

Jack had not seen a Grand National at Aintree for several years, and he was amazed to observe how the place had run down. Iris and Jack wandered through acres of large and cheerless dining rooms, gloomy and desolate in their faded wallpaper. They inched along miles of corridors in the rear of the stands, all faded, old-fashioned, and completely out of date. But there wasn't a single seat in the County Stands of the Members Enclosure from which the view of the whole course wasn't perfect.

The grandstand stretched for half a mile along the side of the track, some of it covered with a glass roof. The day was perfect, a sunny April day, but had it been pouring rain, that glass would have been most appreciated. Behind the stands were the quarters for the jockeys, all in brick, and the stables. In the rear also were the ring for saddling, the rooms for the clerk of the course, the referee, and the other officials.

"Come on," said Iris. "Let's go and see the horses saddled."

The crowd was now large on the concrete before the stands, which sloped gradually upward. The call "Jockeys out," sounded, and the forty riders appeared, each one with a saddle in his arms. The trainers then took the saddles to the saddle box and saddled the horses. When the horses were ready and facing inwards, the trainers led them out in single file in the race-course order. Chester came up to Jack and handed him the reins. Jack refused to take them.

Jack and Iris moved quickly out of the parade ring to catch a glimpse of Quicksilver as he went behind the number board on his way to the course.

Iris turned to Jack. "Tony passed right by and never once noticed me," she said.

"That's concentration for you. See here, we've got seats in a box in the Members Enclosure. Wouldn't you like that?"

"Yes, thanks."

In single file the horses now paraded before the stands, as Iris and he worked through the throng in the underground passage that led to the front.

As they came out, the announcer was saying, "And Number 18, a seven-year-old gelding, owned by Mr. Jack Cobb, of the U.S.A." There was applause from the crowd.

"Why are they clapping?" asked Jack.

"Because they want you to win. Everyone knows what a bad break you had losing your jockey just before the race. Then they know, too, that the horse once belonged to your boy. Hear that. . . ."

The clapping lasted for several minutes. Iris kept looking for Tony as the riders came onto the course. The horses were all mixed up, and the starter needed some time to get them separated and lined up.

Iris had the glasses up. "There he is. I see him now."

"Yes," Jack answered. "I see him too. He's in the second row." Sure enough, there was Tony in his red sash, sitting quietly on Quicksilver in the spring sunshine. The referee called back an unruly horse into line, and without warning the rope dropped.

It was a quarter of a mile to the fence, and all they could distinguish were the backs of the jockeys and the rumps of the horses. Everyone was over the first, and then the second, but at the third a horse tipped the fence, bringing

151

down another, and still a third horse failed to get out of the way. They fell together on the far side of the open ditch.

"Jack!" exclaimed Iris, seizing his hand. The feel and touch of her clasp lifted him, though it was cold as stone.

When Jack Cobb first met Iris Hunting, he had thought she was bossy and not very well mannered. Little by little, however, he realized there was more to her than appeared on the surface, and he changed in his attitude. She had established herself in a tough profession by sheer competence. Her boy was riding in the National, even though she herself dreaded the ordeal. All sorts of people, from dukes and lords on down, turned to her with horses in trouble.

Now he wondered whether he was possibly falling in love with Iris Hunting. He only knew that when she reached for his hand that day the whole world changed.

15

While he stood there, holding on to her hand for dear life, little flickers of doubt passed through Jack's head. No use talking. Tony looked good on the horse, but how would he stand up when confronted by those enormous fences? How would he respond to this test, the toughest and most difficult that any horseman must endure. Choosing Tony was not, indeed, the easiest thing in the world, with the vet bitterly opposed, the head groom lukewarm, and even Chester neutral. But Tony had a quiet strength that was convincing. He had character, like his mother.

These thoughts flooded through him as he stood there, his arm hooked into Iris's. They watched Quicksilver take fence after fence, measuring the jumps just right. He was landing impeccably. Immediately he was down he began to prepare for the next, and he was foot perfect, never a false move or a wrong one. Jack decided that he had made the correct choice of jockey after all.

Now the horse was going for Bechers. Up and over. Then the Canal, where the course turned to the left. Next Valentines, then back toward the stands and the mighty Chair Fence, the biggest of them all. The spectacular Water Jump, in front of the stands, followed. Jack could tell Quicksilver was enjoying himself by the way his ears were pricked as he went on to take fence after fence in perfect form.

The B.B.C. had divided the course into quarters, and a different commentator was announcing each section. In the lead was Ballyhackle, followed closely by a French horse, and with them Sunloch, a horse trained in Ireland. They were now at the far side of the course. As they swept over the fence, Jack raised his glasses to follow them.

And at that precise moment the B.B.C. shifted

from one commentator to another. The new man picked up the horses immediately. "Ballyhackle is down . . . Russian Girl up . . . and over . . . and lands on Lutter . . . now Quicksilver is down. . . . You'll recall he's the American horse who did so well at Cheltenham a fortnight ago. And now the field is off for the next fence . . . with Covert Coat leading by a couple of heads, Spanish Dancer second, and Sunloch third. . . ."

Jack felt Iris's fingers tighten on his arm as a collective sigh went through the crowd. The audible gasp told who was the popular favorite. The spectators wanted Quicksilver to win.

Black despair took possession of Jack. He went over all the efforts of the last six months: everything Chester had worked for, everything Iris had done, Tony's great ride at Cheltenham. All gone, gone as if they never had happened.

Suddenly he heard Iris shouting, "He's still in there! He's still in there! He's still in the race."

Sure enough. They were nearing the stretch before the stands, and there was Tony, cool and imperturbable as ever, running just behind the leaders. By the time they reached the turn in the course to the left, his red sash could be made out plainly. There he was ready to make trouble for anyone. In the excitement of the race, the

B.B.C. announcer had made an error and mistaken Quicksilver for another horse.

The jumping of several fences is not too difficult for a horse. But the jumping of thirty fences in rapid succession at full speed, fourteen of them with wide ditches or brooks on one side, is a severe test. Those who had gone around the course once knew they must attempt to do so again, and with a tired animal. Now the challenge was at hand.

Tony began the second round well back, but he was in a good position to strike. The horse was tiring as were the others, for the pace told on them all. Covert Coat was still in the lead, stubbornly followed by Spanish Dancer and Sunloch, neck and neck. It was anyone's race.

Iris was saying something. Jack hardly heard her.

"Best way to stay out of trouble is to be ahead of it." True, but easier said than done. He jammed his hat on his head, trying vainly to conceal from Iris how he felt. Damn it all, if Tony can keep this up, he'll be in the running. Sure to. Why, he's jumping like a bloody kangaroo. Keep a tight rein on him, lad. That's the thing. I believe he's got all the heart in the world, the boy has.

He isn't his mother's son for nothing. The mere thought gave Jack confidence.

So far, Jack reflected, Tony was doing as well as Stan. Better, because Stan never had tried fences like these. The boy's sense of pace and his understanding of horseflesh were good.

He was at the sixth, the seventh now. Come up, my lovely, and get ready for Valentines. He only balanced him just in time, thank God. A terrific jump, and he's over. Did that well, damn well, he did. He felt the pressure of Iris's hand and squeezed hers back. Now for the Water Jump, one of the worst of its kind in England. He's over, by God he is, and clear of the water too. Jack could have sworn he saw air as the horse leaped that fence.

Two to go, and only a couple of rivals ahead. He'll surely place now. Can't miss. Hello, someone is coming up on the outside. Irish Mail?

"That's Irish Mail, isn't it?" he asked Iris tentatively.

"Yes. A good horse. Won the Irish Grand National last year," she answered.

They were together, coming to the last fence of all. Both over, neck and neck. They were gaining on the leaders, overhauling them rapidly.

There goes Spanish Dancer, falling back slightly . . . and now Sunloch . . . they're almost level with the leader, Covert Coat, 440 yards to the finish. The stands are wild now. They want to see Quicksilver finish in the money. Tony is the coolest man on the course; as usual, he's finishing strongly. But can he win? Will he hold off the others?

At this point Quicksilver showed the stuff and the stamina that was in him. He simply went into high gear, and Tony kept the pressure on the reins fair but steady. Once his head was in front, no question about the winner, and he raced home with a couple of lengths to spare.

Iris did a most un-British thing. She threw her arms around Jack and kissed him. "Oh, Jack, I'm so happy for you. . . ."

Jack picked her up in his arms and swung her around.

She tried to push free. "See here," she said. "They'll all be waiting for you to lead the winner in."

Jack kissed her. "Let them wait," he said. "I'm busy. I'm applying for a post as manager of the Hunting Stable."

She needed a second or two to figure out what

he meant. At first she looked puzzled, and then, before his eyes, that radiant smile appeared. "Oh, that. I rather imagine you've got the job. Nobody else to be considered."

Jack couldn't speak. He put his arm around her and, holding her close, led the way to Quicksilver, who was waiting for them to take him into the winner's circle.